'Tis the Season to Get Married

J.P. Sterling

Contents

1. Charlotte Bradbury   1

2. Nick Briggs   14
    Six months later

3. Charlotte   26
    Four months later

4. Charlotte   43

5. Nick   52

6. Charlotte   58

7. Charlotte   73

8. Nick   81

9. Charlotte   89

10. Nick   100

11. Charlotte   107

12. Nick   111

13. Charlotte   116

Epilogue   126
The next fall . . .

About J.P. Sterling   134

Also By J.P. Sterling   136

One

Charlotte Bradbury

"Do you, Clover, take Beau to be your lawful husband, to have and to hold, until death do you part?" the preacher read from his prayer book.

I do! I desperately tried not to mouth the words. I didn't want anybody to think I was mocking this, because well, it wasn't my wedding. I'm not Clover. I'm Charlotte, the bridesmaid. Again.

And not just a little again.

Again. Again and again.

I was stuck standing up here in front of all these so-happy-for-you people, wearing a brighten-your-day-yellow dress that I'm pretty sure would look better as a bakery tablecloth. I was careful not to squirm. This was Clover's moment, and I didn't want to take any of the attention from her, but boy, budget-heels were a much better idea in theory.

Also, Clover never discussed the flowers with me—not that she had to, as it was clearly her wedding—but the part where I, the bridesmaid, had to hold her bouquet of matching brighten-your-day yellow daisies, was getting a little dicey. She glossed over the detail that I was highly allergic to pollen, and these smellier-than-average daisies were quickly becoming flex-your-face-off-to-avoid-sneezing-during-the-vows daisies.

It started with a light tickle on the tip of my nose. Luckily, I tamed that twitch by pulling the bouquet down further. Good thing I had long arms. Not like spider monkey arms. Let's not get carried away with comparison, but I knew my way around a basketball court.

The tickle subsided for a mere moment, and then it returned. This time with vengeance, sprouting deep roots in the walls of my nose. My gaze skirted to the side where the videographer was zoomed in on us.

If I can hold it for another minute.

This was Clover's moment. *They were about to kiss.*

A spiral inside my nose erupted like a tornado tasked with the job of evacuating all the scent from my nose. Holding my breath was no longer an option and I was about to blow some serious snot.

That couldn't happen!

Out of panic reflex, I chucked the bouquet forward, gritting my teeth when it sailed across the church, only to land in a lady's lap. The crowd started cheering—they obviously thought it was on purpose. Tossing a heel up, I did some weird curtsy thing, trying to act like it *had* been on purpose. I lucked out on that deal, but inside I was still dying.

The tickle receded, but my eyes locked on the happy couple just as their lips met. I clamped my jaw hard with everything I had to avoid ruining their perfect moment. I was happy for her, my boss. My friend who I got to watch fall in love with her client, Beau Tucker. I was truly happy for her. So happy. I felt happy. Okay, maybe I was a little jealous. But mostly I was, er, happy.

Good thing tears were common at weddings.

"So, do I want to be in a serious relationship?" I nodded in answer to Nick' question, setting my seconds-after-another-friend's-perfect-wedding-mocktail glass down to clear my hands so I could better defend myself to my best friend, Nick. We were sitting near a window at the bar in Harbor Inn and lodge, the *same* lodge where my three best friends held their destination weddings.

They all chose the town of Mapleton because, "it held the perfect winter wonderland background for a beautiful Christmas wedding." Mapleton was so charming it was named the number-one spot to have a Christmas wedding. I'd bought so many weekend packages to stay here as a bridesmaid, I was pretty sure I deserved a free upgraded bride package any day now—I just needed to find a groom.

"I do." My adrenaline ticked up—like way up—all the way up to my neck. I continued to use my hands to illustrate my point, something I always did when I got emotional. Placing my flattened palm on my chest to stifle the rush, I continued, "Do I want to go to vineyards and apple orchards?"

"—I love apple orchards," Nick cut in. "They have the best hard cider."

"Cheers to apple orchards!" I pinched the stem of my glass between my fingers, and tapped it with his, then lowered it to my lips so I could take another generous sip of my mocktail, made with their famous poinsettia garnish. As I came up for air, I finished my sentence right where I had left off. "And hayrides with pumpkin spice lattes, sharing fluffy blankets that are perfectly coordinated to match our turtleneck sweaters, and do all the other insanely cute stuff?" I paused, but did not let him answer. He didn't need to tell me how he was feeling because I already knew. We were both tired of people acting as if I didn't know *all* our friends were marrying off at increasing speeds. That didn't sound like something I should be upset about, but no matter how much they insisted they would still make time for a night out, one-by-one they disappeared into the baby-raising abyss.

I shifted in my seat, scooting closer to the edge. Sure, I'd get an invite to birthday parties, or a family picnic—and I enjoy supporting my friends in that way—but it was *painful* to always show up alone, when all I wanted was to be able to do what they were doing.

I saw all my friends getting married.

Of course, I saw them!

"I do," I rambled out. "I want all of that. I want to get married in a country church to my best friend. We'll start a business together, a flower store, or Bed and Breakfast, and do all the things together while popping out another baby every other year. It's what I want *most* in life. But do I want to go on dates with every loser I barely know, just to suffer through hours of awkward conversations, only to find out he is a player like the rest of them?" I sealed my lips tightly and wagged my head back and forth.

No words are needed.

"I know what you mean." Nick leaned forward as he picked up my comment perfectly, like I knew he would. He always understood what I was going through. "I'm no Michelangelo's David but I want to find *one* woman who likes to cuddle on the couch, without having to twist her face into fourteen versions of duck lips so she can take the perfect ego-feeding selfie." He gestured toward me. "Is that too much to ask?"

"Oh, I hate selfies." I seethed, remembering his recollection of his last date. "When I'm on a date, I want to look at the other person, not stare at an isolated reflection of myself. I mean, I've been doing that long enough."

"Agreed!"

"Is it too much to ask my fairy Godmother to hurry and change a pumpkin into a carriage to transport me to the ball to meet my prince already?" I whined, but it came out forcefully like it was wrestling with a groan.

"Well, I hate to inform you." Nick rubbed his chin, cueing his transition to an armchair therapist, "nor do I want to be *that* guy who points this out, but you used your pumpkin in a latte for the hayride. I don't think you can ride in your pumpkin and drink it, too." His phone dinged, drawing his attention. "Uh, I'm sorry, Char. This is work." He placed the phone next to his ear, tacking on, "This will just be a second."

Grinning, I dropped my eyes back to my drink, rotating the glass slowly with my thumb and forefinger, wistfully dreaming of my prince. *What in the world was taking him so long?* I was at the stage in life, where I would be okay with backup prince number one—or even number two—if he had his act together.

I wasn't even sure if I believed in soulmates. At this point, I would be perfectly fine making a home with my soul neighbor—just as long as he didn't hog the covers at night, or listen to talk radio in the car. Well . . . technically, I could always bring earbuds. Maybe I could make an exception for the talk radio if he didn't complain about my bare feet being on the dash while I rode shotgun. *They always get too sweaty with shoes on!* They much preferred riding in the daylight.

Yeah, talk radio for a barefoot swap. That seemed like a logical compromise. Oh! And he'd have to listen to "Blue Christmas" by Elvis, on repeat, from Thanksgiving to Christmas, while also singing harmony, but he could totally have the other forty-eight weeks after that for his talk radio. Except for the obvious Elvis week where "Can't Help Falling in Love" would have to blast on all six speakers with the window rolled down to hear it outside of the car so we could dance under the stars—but that would be a given. If I had to explain dancing under the stars to any man, he definitely wasn't soul neighbor material.

Actually, since I'd been waiting so long, scratch everything except the dancing under the stars.

Dancing under the stars was a very reasonable condition that should be a cinch to finagle. Then, off to happily-ever-after land, and I wouldn't have to spend the rest of my life alone.

Nick set his phone screen down, leaning back into our conversation. "Sorry about that. Where were we?"

"I don't know," I started, ready to give up on love entirely so I could be finished dating. "Find me a dude who needs a maid but promises to take care of me forever—or something close—and I'd be happy to fill that role. I want to be done with dating." I pushed out my bottom lip and plopped my chin to rest in my palm. "It's such a waste of time."

Nick stretched one arm up and dropped it to scratch the back of his head. "I feel like I can put in another year, or two, tops, just to see if there are any stragglers who like to cuddle, but I'm going to end up where you are here shortly if all I get are duck lips."

"Another year and you'll be thirty," I commented, letting my eyes smack him with that reality.

"It's *adomania*." Nick's words came out soft, barely above a whisper, while he stared wide-eyed at me.

"Is that another word for a birthday?" I hiked a brow, letting a smile take over my face as I marveled at his rare talent for knowing the most unknown words that perfectly summed up every conversation. I called him the word whisperer. He hated that nickname, but that didn't stop him from going out of his way to find the most obscure words.

"Nah, not birthday." He blinked a couple of times as if he was trying to refocus on our conversation and then planted his gaze back on me. "It means your future is coming too quickly."

I let the definition ring over, and I had to admit he'd done it again. He'd summed up this entire conversation with one word. "It's perfect, 'adomania.'" My voice floated, as if it was still holding awe. He nodded gently, and I nodded back, our smiles synchronizing before I added, "Can you imagine how hard dating is going to be in our thirties?"

"I can imagine it will be pathetic—"

"So pathetic," I finished his thought like always. "Here we are, two amazing people,"—I straighten my spine, feeling an ego boost coming— "and nobody wants to spouse us up."

"Everyone must be blind." His words were laced with a low sputtering chuckle.

"Obviously." My eyes made a giant arc around the top of my lid as I strove for the most perfect eye roll ever. "I mean, look at you," I gestured to him with both hands. "You're like what? The most genius CPA on the planet?"

He shrugged only one shoulder, as if he were more-or-less accepting that as a compliment. "More like an office manager."

"Just call yourself a human calculator with all those skills." My words were starting to slur now. I didn't care because I had a point to prove, even if I was overtired, beyond the point of exhaustion and so emotional. I licked my lips, trying to remember what that point was . . . I wasn't sure, so I took another sip of my drink and stared at him until he came into focus. Then I remembered! "Oh, yeah, so what do you make a year, six figures?"

"Low six."

"Right!" I pointed at him accusingly because it would make him laugh. "You're rich!"

He snickered, but I continued as I still had a point to prove. I clumsily gestured at him again. "And you're buff! I've seen you with your shirt off, and you have two shadows of abs in there. Sometimes." My own laughter cut off my words as I giggled intensely and fondly looked back at my best friend. He was laughing, too. Not looking even slightly offended because he knew it was true.

Wrapping my fingers around the stem of my mocktail glass again, I lifted it to my lips and finished the rest, before setting it down, and seeing my glass was now empty. It was a little blurry from the tears, which had been sitting in the back of my eyes all night. I could mostly see it, and it was most definitely empty.

I was tired of being a glass-is-empty person. It was painful. Part of what one gets out of life is what they put into it. At some point, I would have to accept the plight I was given. It was then I made my decision. Letting out a sigh steeped in desperation, I put a voice to my decision, "If I'm not married—or at least engaged by Christmas—I'm forever giving up on dating—for eternity."

Nick quirked a skeptical brow. "This Christmas? That's eleven months."

"'Tis the season to get married."

"I know you want a Christmas wedding by why this year? It's so soon."

"I'm wasting time, caring about dating. I could use all energy for a new hobby." I pursed duck lips to remind him of his own fate, then tacked on, "Want to join me? We could make a pact."

"I don't know." He nervously scratched the back of his head. "I mean, I really like to cuddle."

I glared at him through my one good eye, which was less blurry than the other one. I picked up my glass to take another drink, but found it empty, which made me sad. I didn't want to be sad because I had a plan. Or more like a pact, and I was trying to snatch a partner for my pact. I flashed him more duck lips and said, "Quack," which sent us both into another rush of laughter.

"Okay," his tone lowered, and he latched his eyes onto mine. "I'm done with duck lips. If I am not engaged by Christmas, I'll be done dating too, and we can do hayrides together."

"Wait." My eyes skirted the room, trying to see where that idea came from. "What did you say?"

"I said, I'm in. I agree with your pact. I'll give up if I'm not engaged by Christmas."

"No, no, no." I wagged my finger in the air. "What was that other part?"

"We can do hayrides together?" His voice teetered up, ending his statement as a question.

"Together?" I hiked a brow at him, feeling his vibes. "Are you saying, when we give up trying to find other people, we will just be together?"

"Well, I mean, if we are both single . . . it makes sense that we hang out, no?"

"Wait for a second. I'm getting an idea." I leaned forward, trying to pull him into my excitement. "If we aren't married by Christmas, then *we should get married to each other!*"

I could see him mouth the words "marry each other," but it wasn't audible. Then his eyes sprang wide as they hooked mine. "Yeah, that's the best idea ever!"

"I know!" I sprang to my feet, exclaiming, "I'm getting matching turtlenecks just in case! What's your size?"

"Large," he answered in a definitive tone and added, "I'll book the honeymoon suite here at the lodge—just in case."

"Right." I nodded, finding it perfectly acceptable. Then I leaned forward, extending a playful fist toward him. Somewhere over the years of wasting time together, we had accidentally made our secret handshake, and I was ready to deploy it. "Okay, Nick this is it. I swear if I'm not married by Christmas, I will meet you here in Mapleton, and marry you."

He balled his fist and pushed it out toward me for a bump, then we both made a half heart with our fingers and connected it in the middle. Nick didn't waste a second to confirm, "Deal."

Two

Nick Briggs

Six months later

It was a random Friday night in July, and I was out with some of the guys from our office softball league. We completed a two-day tournament, which was actually pretty fun. I hit the ball every time I batted, and I also didn't drop any I caught, helping our team come in second place. For a group of guys who'd never played together before, and many who'd never played much at all because we were more "nerds" than jocks, we were stoked about that.

We found a round high-top table in the back corner of the pub and piled around it. My boss, Trey Michaels, sat one seat over from me, leaving the seat immediately next to me open. He gestured to the seat, "Atalie is going to be joining us in a minute. If that's okay, I'm saving her a seat."

"That's cool." I had to almost holler over the celebratory voices of the group mixed with the crowd noise. I would never classify myself as an introvert like most of the guys

I worked with, because I was social, but the bar scene was never my favorite.

"Or, do you have someone coming," Trey nearly yelled again. "Because I can move down one more?"

"No," I said as a victory cheer erupted across the table.

Trey must not have heard me because he repeated his question, this time enunciating each word more, almost shouting it at me. "Do. You. Have. A. Date. Coming!"

Of course, when the boss shouts, people listen, especially since he never shouts, and it's completely out of his character. The side conversations around the table dropped off, all eyes fled to Trey screaming about my dating life. I don't normally get embarrassed. Not around these guys anyway. We worked together every day, and they all know I'm single, but it felt as if every pair of eyes in the entire bar was on me now. "No." My single word answer was extra sharp, hoping to send the message that I wasn't open to discussing my dating life, or lack thereof any further. I tugged on the bill of my ballcap, pulling it down low, and dug into the bowl of pretzels in front of me. Everybody went right back into their conversations, and more of their dates joined us, filling every other chair with a beautiful woman.

I pulled out my phone, saw I had a Goodreads update, notifying me that Charlotte had updated her book recommendations. Her date must have been awful, because she was home early, and updating books on Friday night. Who does that?

Me: How was your set up with Salsa king?

Charlotte: Don't ask.

Me: Okay. What are you doing home so early tonight?

Charlotte: He brought me a jar of salsa!!

Me: Like as a gift?

Charlotte: Yeah, like I said, "Nice to meet you" and he held it out like a peace offering. I had no idea what to say. I didn't want to admit that I had Googled him and already knew he owned a salsa empire. He didn't add any explanation, so it looked like a strange gift.

Me: Was it good salsa?

Atalie, Trey's wife, took her seat next to me, as a gust of wind came in through the open window beside me, hinting at a summer storm. Even though I loved the smell, the humidity was thick. "Hi Nick." She smiled sweetly at me, as she hung her purse on the back of the stool. "Great game."

"Thanks. Did you see my home run?" I pulled my lips into a welcoming smile. Out of all my friends' wives, Atalie was the nicest one. I was convinced it was because she had such a hard life before meeting Trey. She was actually a young widow, single mother who Trey had hired to work as his maid. She clearly hit the jackpot marrying Trey, one of the richest men in the city, but it never changed her personality. She was more down to earth than most people I knew.

"I did!" Her smile spread wider across her face. "I really thought you guys would win. It's a shame to lose right at the bottom of the ninth."

"We'll get them next year." I was all smack talk, but it made for more fun conversation. Someone across the table asked her a question, and she turned to reply. I dropped my gaze back to my phone and read Charlotte's text.

Charlotte: Of course it was amazing. It would be fantastic on your enchiladas.

Me: Nice! At least we know where to get good salsa. What did you guys do?

Charlotte: We were at my friend's house for dinner, and the power went out. We painfully sat in the dark and the only thing he talked about was his stupid tomato farms.

Me: Awkward. So, not going to work out for you then?

Charlotte: Hard no.

I chuckled. Not because I lacked empathy because I could visualize how awkward that had been, but it was another one of those dates that Charlotte seemed prone to. She had the worst luck.

Me: That's too bad.

Charlotte: It's okay, I have another date next week with a cop. And let's just say he's handsome. That

should go better. What about you? Have you met anyone interesting lately?

My chest tightened. She had been going on an awful lot of dates lately. Even more than usual, and although I encouraged her, it always felt odd to hear about her preferences. I didn't feel comfortable talking about that stuff with *too* much detail. I thought about how to answer her question as I looked around the bar, crammed with people. I hadn't really done an inventory. There had to be a single woman in here somewhere, but I didn't even want to try.

Me: Tacenda

Charlotte: What in the world does that mean?

Me: Better left unsaid.

Charlotte: Just tell me.

Me: More duck lips.

I didn't want her to think I wasn't trying to find someone else to marry. The truth was, Charlotte was all I had hoped for, but I never had the chance to tell her that.

The moment was never right.

As I set my phone on the table, I spotted a bar pizza that had been dropped off. I helped myself to a slice of something with way too many vegetables on it. *Who eats vegetables in a bar?*

I found myself smirking about Charlotte's date, recalling how the salsa jar was an object of peacekeeping in our home. Whenever my mom was mad at my dad, she would go into these silly fits where she'd ignore him. They never lasted long, because Dad had figured out her need for salsa was more important than her need to hold a grudge. Dad would sneak into the kitchen and tighten the lid of the salsa jar so tightly that my mom couldn't even open the lid with a vice grip. It always made me laugh because it played out the same every time. Mom would mutter about how "This time he wasn't going to get his way." I'd snicker from the other side of the kitchen counter, and she'd wag her finger at me. "Nicholas, my son. Did you see your father do this to me again? He tightened my salsa. Who does that?"

At about that time, she would move to the sink and run the jar under hot water. When that didn't work, she'd pull a blunt knife out of the drawer and tap the lid in random places. By now, her muttering was in full-blown Spanish, and I was also in a laughter fit. She'd glare at me and shake her finger again. "Nicholas, my baby boy, if you ever have a wife, don't mess with her salsa."

I'd roll my eyes because, *of course,* I was never getting married. I was a late bloomer when it came to liking girls. Or maybe it just had more to do with the girls at my school not being my type? Nonetheless, I remember constantly feeling my face burn when she'd suggest me having a wife.

If it weren't for the example I had from my dad, I might still cringe at the thought of marriage. He was the rock to our whole family. He had impeccable timing with my mom too. Just as she was about to go into a fit over her salsa, he would appear in the doorway. Like a superhero he wouldn't even speak but silently held out his hand to reach for the jar.

Still stubborn, my mom avoided his gaze when she passed the jar. Her whole demeanor changed when she heard the lid make that air-popping noise, announcing it was open. Her lips would curl, and she would let out an airy laugh aimed more at herself than anything. By the time Dad handed her the jar back, she willingly gave him a hug, and their fights were over. Not that they ever had any big fights. It was always usual marriage stuff as far as I knew, but this make-up routine was so cute and perfect.

On the surface, it may have seemed mean for my dad to do that, but he told me once he would do anything he could to make sure Mom never had to go to sleep mad at him. I don't think I fully understood how humble that was until a few years ago.

I stared out the window. It was crazy living in New York. The traffic never stopped, and everywhere I looked were crowds of people. I was never alone, but it's actually where I feel the most alone. I always thought I'd have settled down by now, but maybe, my parents' marriage ruined me a little. Maybe my expectations were too high, but none of the girls I'd dated were smitten with gestures like that.

Or maybe it was because none of the women I dated were Charlotte.

Whenever Charlotte was near, she had this acute effect on my body, making my heart ramp up to unnatural speeds. It was a struggle just to stand beside her, and not run out of breath. I wasn't even out of shape, running three miles daily. It was just her.

It had been ten years since that fateful day when I first saw her. Like a scene in a movie, she was standing on the corner of Main Street in Mapleton, my hometown. One foot was bare, and she was holding a heeled leather boot in one hand.

Serendipitous perfection.

Even with her broken shoe, and sorrowful expression, she was the quintessential American beauty. I would have felt compelled to talk to her without her situation, but since she was in distress, I had an excuse to say something to her. Tipping my head to her shoe, I said in my best pleased-to-meet-you voice, "May I help you?"

Her emerald eyes had risen to meet mine, and I would be lying if I said I didn't feel an instant attraction. The early December air was chilly, but it was one of those rare days when the sun broke the Vermount overcast, and the apricity magnified her beauty, as well as fueled my courage. She offered an amused smile, but it didn't align with the stressed inflections in her eyes, when she said, "I slipped off the curb and my heel caught on it." A delicate bell-like tone lingered in the air. Her voice flowed like honey with musical words that were a gentle invitation swiftly warming my heart. I'm not embellishing the memory one bit. I was instantly *enamored* by her.

"I don't suppose this little town even has a shoe store?" she asked in her smooth voice.

I shook my head, thankful for the perfect opportunity to swoop in to help this gorgeous lady. "But we have a general store, and I can glue your heel back on."

The perfect canvas between her brows wrinkled as she pinned a perplexed expression on her face. "You don't have to—"

"I insist." I motioned to the store across the street, while doing my best not to act too eager. "The store's right there, and I could never let a lady walk around shoeless."

"In that case, I accept. Thank you." Her perfectly groomed brows lifted, and she reached her delicate hand out, offering a handshake. "I'm Charlotte."

"I'm Nick." When I took her hand in mine, a shot of adrenaline slammed into my heart. At first, I thought it had to have been the triple shot of espresso latte I had drunk, but I didn't feel it in my head, like from a caffeine buzz. Instead, I felt it in my chest. I had this strange sensation wash through me that said my life was about to change.

I just wasn't exactly sure how.

I'd never had the experience of meeting someone and instantly feeling a connection to them, despite only having minimal interaction. However, that's what happened. People say instalove, but that wasn't it. Instalove, to me, always seemed more hormones and lust, and all-in, or nothing. This was more innocent than instalove. It was the tiny first impression, the mere beginning of love, if you will. Rubbing my chin, I search for the perfect word. *Forelsket.* Yep, that's the word, it's that innocent euphoria you experience when first falling in love.

That whole afternoon played out in slow motion. I still remember every moment as we bimbled around Mapleton. At the general store, I offered to treat her to anything she wanted. I was mostly being silly and wanting to impress her, but inside I prayed she didn't pick something crazy expensive. I had just moved to New York and working on temp wages. Being flat broke had put a damper on my dating life, but something inside me told me she'd be worth whatever expense she selected. To my surprise—and my budget-heart approval—she grabbed the biggest bag of cotton candy, and strapped a huge boisterous smile on her face as she headed to the cashier and allowed me to pay.

I fixed Charlotte's shoe. Well, more like I nervously slathered way too much glue on it until I gave up trying to make that stick. Not before I made a huge mess of my sleeve. I tried playing it cool by rolling it up, which ended up being a terrible idea, because I forgot I had done that until I tried to do laundry. It was super glued together, so much so, that I ended up throwing that shirt away. Anyway, back to the shoe. I returned to the store for a nail and hammer, which I drove through her heel, and thankfully that worked like a charm.

We found a bench outside. She daintily sat with that giant bag of rainbow cotton candy on her lap. I had expected her to politely graze off the top while she ate in a lady-like manner. Instead, she went all in, whipping out whole handfuls, and seemed so ferociously engrossed in eating it that she didn't notice I was staring at her. Contrary to her dainty and feminine exterior, from her velvet day dress to her loose curls, she flat hogged out. Boy—I was mesmerized by how she threw caution to the wind when it came to that bag of fluffed sugar. I pinched my lips, trying to contain any laughter, because I didn't want to ruin her joy, which was so evident from the deeply dented dimples on her cheek.

She got up to wash her hands in the ladies' room, but when I peeked over my shoulder, she was licking her fingers clean. Maybe there was something wrong with me that I wasn't grossed out by this, but all I could think was, *I could seriously date her.*

She came back, and we spent the next few hours walking around town, talking about anything and everything. That night, I gave Charlotte a piece of my heart, but she quickly moved me into the friend zone. Year after year, she had returned to Mapleton on Christmas break. She seemed to always have a wedding to attend, but never had anything but *friendly* smiles for me.

I finished my memory right as I swallowed the last of my pizza and realized a couple of the guys had already taken off. If I didn't want to get caught in the storm, it would be wise for me to leave too. I got up from my chair, flashed a wave, and called, "That's it for me tonight." A ripple of goodbyes flowed, and I left.

I had one niggling thought on my mind. The one that always plagued me.

I'm not a scientist, a psychologist, or an expert of any sort, but I'm convinced the most screwed up thing that can ever happen to you is falling in love first, and having to wait, forever wondering if she'll *ever fall for you, too*.

Three
Charlotte
Four months later

Me: I'm logging into my watch party. It's your turn to pick a movie.

Setting my remote down on my coffee table, I leaned back, tugged a fleece blanket up, and snuggled it. Nick and I had started this Sunday night movie watch party thing as soon as the technology had allowed it.

Nick: Go ahead and pick a movie you want to watch, and get it started. Be right there. I just burnt my pizza. I want to clean this up quick.

Me: Pizza tonight? Yum. I have the usual popcorn and Nerds.

Nick: Well, it was pizza. Now it's more like toast.

I picked my remote back up and scrolled through the available movies. Nick preferred comedies. I was a classic romance girl, which meant romcoms usually won. There wasn't anything newly released that we needed to see, and all the titles that rolled through seemed anticlimactic. Disney Princess it is! I clicked on Tangled, and stared at my phone, waiting for the reaction.

Nick: Again?

I snickered, not feeling even a little bit of a need to defend my selection because I couldn't even count how many times I had watched every Adam Sandler movie. Instead of responding to his reaction, I pushed play on the movie, and changed the subject.

Me: You didn't cancel your reservation for Mapleton, did you?

Nick: No, why? Your date not go well?

Me: It was fine. He would have been husband material, but he took me to this pub, and it ended up being the pub Jon always used to go to. You know I don't drink but I didn't complain. So, the second I walked in, Jon found me, and of course, he hovered over our table, talking the whole time.

Nick: What? You spent your date talking to your ex-boyfriend?!

Me: He didn't know he was an ex.

Nick: You do know that is a terrible thing to do on a date, right?

Me: Yep. After twenty minutes, he said he was going to drive me home.

Nick: You are lucky he was that nice, I would have left you.

Me: I never said I was good at dating. If I were, I wouldn't still be doing it after all these years. I mean it, Nick. I'm about to give up. I hope you weren't joking about our marriage pact.

Nick: Never.

Me: I'm helping my boss this weekend by watching her sister. I'm not going to even think about men.

Once Rapunzel got put in her tower, I got up to use the restroom. One of the advantages to having every scene memorized is that you can do other things and never get lost in the plot. I had a sudden craving for hot chocolate and found my way into the kitchen. While I waited for my teapot to heat up, I texted Nick again.

Me: Nick, are you still there?

Nick: Yeah, just watching the mean old mother climb up. It's prosperous to think no one ever saw her do that. I mean, it doesn't look suspicious at all!

Me: So, about Mapleton, I'm thinking I should book a flight now. Are you going to be there? I know we joke around a lot.

Nick: Already got my flight.

I set my phone on the counter and prepared my hot chocolate. Meeting in Mapleton is what we did every Christmas. He'd fly home from New York to visit his folks, and I always made time during my Christmas break to meet him. I loved his little Christmas-perfect town. Living my whole life in Texas, I had to take a yearly trip to see snow. We'd enter some whimsical Christmas village, and it did everything to put me in the Christmas spirit.

This year felt different.

Clearly, it was the marriage pact joke we had been tossing around, but sometimes it seemed Nick's words had double meaning, leaving me wondering if maybe it wasn't a joke?

I bit down on one side of my lip, letting my mind replay our conversations.

It was a joke, right?

I mean, he wouldn't actually want to get married. Guys hate marriage, right? Hence why I haven't gotten there yet. He was merely blowing smoke to make me feel better about not finding a husband yet. We practically shared a brain. Nick understood how much I wanted to settle down and have a big family. I wasn't being greedy. It was the opposite, as I just had so much love to give. I was raised as an only child, and never wanted for anything material-wise. My dad did the best a single dad could do, staying career-oriented to provide, but I was left with nannies—*a lot*.

Nannies who were friendly as they tended to all my needs. Still, they only stayed a year, and then left to go back to college after crossing me off their life experience list. It sounds petty because I had a great childhood and don't deserve to have a list of grievances. And I don't, but I'm in charge of my future. I want, more than anything, to have a home filled with love and people who stay, not because they are paid to be there, but because it's home.

I placed my mug on a tray and dug through the pantry for some chips before heading back to the living room. When I tried to get back into the movie, I couldn't help but think about Nick. This marriage banter was clearly making me a little batty. Maybe it wasn't a good idea to make light of something I wanted the most in life? It would be best to text him and tell him I was excited to see him, but I wasn't expecting anything more.

Surely, he wasn't expecting anything more?

Before I could talk myself out of it, I texted him again.

Me: So, like the whole deal with Mapleton. Are we just going to hang out? I'm fine if that's what you want. Actually, right now I just need a weekend away.

I must have been more tired than I thought because I nodded off before I got his reply. A few hours later, I woke up to a glowing TV screen, and a text from him.

Nick: By the way, I wouldn't have left you at the bar. That was a joke.

"That was a diversion, but why?" I asked myself as I set my phone back down, mulling over why he didn't answer my question. I didn't dwell on it too long, though, before I rolled over to go back to sleep, pretending to not feel my gut twist.

"Is that my favorite daughter?" A deep voice rang from the old two-story farmhouse doorstep early the next morning.

My eyes landed on my father who stood over six feet tall, even at sixty years old. Dad's entire family was tall. Dad claimed it was from drinking black coffee. When I was little, I believed him and would proudly drink coffee at the breakfast table with him. Of course, he didn't know I snuck three sugar packets into my cup when he wasn't looking. It wasn't until I got older that I realized height had nothing to do with the coffee; instead we were blessed with tall genes. By then, it was too late, and I already had a full-blown caffeine addiction. Still, to this day, I credit my spry old Dad for that fault.

I opened my arms and received a tight hug where I fit perfectly under his chin. It was seriously the best hug possible to fit like this. "Hey, Dad." I grazed my cheek momentarily on his chest, feeling cozy next to his red flannel shirt. Safe.

"It's good to see you." He patted my back and pulled away, ushering me through the open door with the wave of his hand. "I got coffee in the pot, waiting for you."

"Ah, thanks." I forced a pleasantly surprised tone, but we both knew I wasn't amazed. It was the game we played. I continued inside, shutting the old-farm house door behind me by giving it more than a gentle nudge, and unwrapped the gray wool scarf from my neck.

This house had been my grandmother's and the home my dad grew up in. He'd inherited it when I was just a baby. Since my dad wasn't one for décor, it mostly still looked as if a nineteen fifties housewife had designed it. With everything from the robin's egg blue cabinets to yellow and white curtains hanging on the window. The one thing he had updated was the table. Though, he didn't buy a new one, but instead made one from reclaimed barn wood, claiming this table was more masculine and comfortable than the little metal retro one we used to have.

"Just black, right?" He hobbled over to the counter, favoring his bad knee like he always did. The only explanation I'd ever been given about his knee was a service wound, but I'd suspected it had more to do with his years of playing catcher in the Marine softball team. Either way, it's how I always remembered him, hobbling around, too stubborn to use a cane.

He grabbed my favorite Christmas mug, the one with a picture of the Mapleton Christmas tree on it. Every year when I went to Mapleton, I asked him what he wanted for a souvenir. He'd always request, "another mug for my collection." I'd put money on him having more Mapleton mugs than anyone who actually lived there. He was practical when it came to gifts, and everything he did.

"Always." A smile budded on my lips, pinning back the chuckle I always had for my sweet dad.

As he set my cup, he butted my mug right up next to the sugar bowl, and dramatically turned his back. "I just filled the sugar—for no reason at all."

I pretended to be covertly dumping sugar into my cup, but we both knew my secret was out years ago.

After filling a mug for himself, he scooted a chair out next to mine and sat down. Sitting straight like a drill sergeant was watching, because he never let any of his old habits fall to the wayside. He was a *proud* ex-Marine. In fact, once, I introduced him to a friend as ex-*military*, and I got a going-on-thirty-minute ear full about how he was not military. He was a Marine. *There's a difference.*

"You look pretty," he said, but not in the positive way you would expect words like that to sound. Instead, it emulated to a T the role of a "suspicious ex-Marine." "You got a date?"

"I wish I had a date, but I'm babysitting for my boss." I blew on my coffee before taking a generous sip.

"I see." His chin raised and lowered the way he always did before he'd give me parental advice I didn't ask for. "It's been a while since you found someone to take you out—"

"Dad," I cut him off as this was so cringy to discuss with him. He was old-fashioned when it came to dating, as he still thought guys should wear suits, open every door, and always pay the entire bill for *every* date. When I was in high school, he enforced the rule that the guy had to ask me out, and he refused to let me call any boy first. I may still be holding onto that memory as the sole excuse for never having a date to the prom.

It wasn't until I got older I learned a way around the rule, and I started getting regular dates. I never did call a guy first, but I had no shame in casually, and sometimes more directly, giving a cute boy my number and *asking* him to call. Dad didn't know about that, though; he'd break the ceiling if he did. It's not like it was a secret, but I learned years ago that he'd never understand how different dating these days was. All the men with old fashioned values were *dead*. "It's fine," I said as nonchalantly as I could. "I've been busy with work—"

His lips caved down, as he clearly wasn't trying to mask his true feelings. "That's your first problem. Guys don't like it when women spend too much time working." He wasn't taking a lecture tone, but I didn't have the stomach to be told why I was failing.

I knew I was failing!

I spent a hundred thousand dollars to find a husband! All I got was a stupid piece of paper that said something lame like "Communications Degree." I framed it and hung it on my wall, but I didn't want a piece of paper; *I want a ring!* "It's fine." I placed my palm over his freckled hand, squeezing it as lovingly as I could, gritted my teeth, and said, "It doesn't bother me—"

"Well, it should." He imposingly flung his other hand toward me in the same manner he always did when I wasn't living my life his way. "If you don't meet a nice man soon, you won't have time to properly date before you get married because your clock is ticking."

"Its *fine*." My voice came out edged in a bit of a growl, as I couldn't have this conversation today—or any day—because it was beyond awkward. I never held onto any sadness about not being raised by my mother, but it was times like these that I felt a mentor was missing. Someone to guide me without the drill-sergeant tone, while also sweetly helping my dad to see his helping wasn't "helpful."

He gave me his stern eye lock and went on, "I think—"

"I'm getting married!" I blurted out and held his eyes steady, terrified of something dreadful happening. I hadn't planned on telling him—or anyone—about the marriage pact, but it had been in the front of my brain for weeks and somehow slipped out. As I waited in the stony silence, I listened to my words continue to thump around my head, and realized I would need to back that proclamation up with some details.

Dad's eyes narrowed with obvious skepticism, but before he could press me for specifics I rattled out, "I never told you because I, well, it's really new, like *so new*, and *we* wanted to elope, but yeah, I'm getting married this next weekend!" I pulled my lips into the in-love smile and squeaked, "Isn't it great?"

I wanted to duck under the table to hide from what was coming next. Dad was smart, and he knew I had always wanted a big, perfect wedding since the day I was three. There was no way this would make any sense to him, because it didn't even make sense to *me*. I clamped down hard on my lip, waiting for him to call my bluff.

Why did I even bring this up? Surely, it won't get me out of his interrogation but will only bring more!

"I don't know if I could agree to that." He leaned closer, as if inspecting my face for clues of deception. "I haven't heard anything about a guy you're courting."

Courting. I flashed my eyes heavenward. *Are we back in the Renaissance?*

"You know of him. It's Nick, my friend I meet for Christmas every year," I divulged, thankful I had so much knowledge of Nick, I could answer questions about him for days. "We didn't really date, because it's long distance. It just came up." I blew a breath, letting my gaze fall to the floor, as I struggled to make this all sound not insane. I tacked on, "He works in an office. He's from Vermont but lives in New York, and he's a huge Jets fan."

"I'm going to need to meet him." His cadence sounded more like a question than a statement.

"You totally can," I said reassuringly as I pushed my sleeves back, trying to let some air in. Suddenly I was feeling a tad warm. "You will . . . meet him. Sometime. We were so excited to get married and start our lives together we couldn't wait to plan a big day." I clumsily elbowed him while I tacked on a grin. "As you said, my clock's ticking."

He stared off into the room, letting the silence linger. I was about to start blubbering out more details, but he pulled his gaze back to lock on mine, and I sucked in a hard breath. Moisture in his steel blue eyes. My dad, the *Marine*, had tears in his eyes. His voice came out hushed, "I don't believe my baby girl is finally getting married."

I tugged my lips into a toothy grin, feeling the guilt of lying to my dad take hold of me but I managed to squeak out, "Yeah, isn't it fantastic."

He reached out, placing his arm around me, squeezing me into a loving hug, and pinning me tightly. My dad, the *Marine*, was getting emotional!

"It's not the way I'd imagined it," he whispered, but since his mouth was close to my ear, I heard him perfectly. "I would have hoped to be able to walk you down the aisle, but if it's what you want, I'll give you my blessing."

"It is." My voice was weak, afraid he could decipher my untruthfulness.

He did that crazy, tell-tale thing they do in movies where people blink, and lightly touch their eye like they have a loose eyelash, but everybody knows they are fighting back a tear. Instead of getting mad about the deception, it makes everyone in the audience cry sooo much harder.

I wasn't on the verge of crying, though. Not even close because I wasn't actually getting married. Okay, maybe I had a small tear.

"I've been holding onto something," he started, but then stopped to take a dramatic swallow, which did not affect the sting in my eye! "I have something for your wedding day and since I won't be there, I'd like to give it to you now."

"I don't—" I tried to shake my head no, but the look on my father's face was one of joy, mixed with pride, and wrapped up in love. *I can't break his heart now!* I could come up with a left-at-the-altar story later for when I came home without a husband, but right at this moment, I saw how much this meant to him. Swallowing my guilt, I smiled sweetly back at him and said, "I'd be honored to get any gift from you."

My dad wasn't ever much of a giver when it came to material items. He was a *pull yourself up by your bootstraps and pay your own way* guy. Even for birthdays and Christmas I never got anything extravagant. A replenishment of socks, maybe some pajamas and books, or a single DVD or doll I had on my wish list. Gifts were always practical, and just in time, so this seemed odd, especially since I hadn't even come close to getting engaged. That he said he had planned something and even saved it for years for my wedding was so far from his character, my entire interest was piqued, and I followed him up to his room.

I slowed my steps as I passed by my old room, still pre-served exactly how'd I left it, with Justin Bieber posters on the walls and giant fake sunflowers shoved in every available space. I cringed, thinking the least he could do was shut the door or better yet remodel it into an office.

He waved me inside his room, saying, "It's right in here."

Pausing against the door, my curiosity was full speed when he opened the bi-fold closet doors, passing over his rows of pressed suits and sweaters until he got all the way to the end and retrieved a hanger sealed with a thick garment bag that hung to the floor. It was beige, plain and had matched the dull wall paint. It blended in so much I had never noticed it hanging there, even though I did recall the many times I—in my younger days—had hidden in his closet for hide-and-seek.

He carried the garment bag with two hands—one hold-ing the hanger and the other hand preventing the bot-tom from dragging on the floor—as he walked it over to his king-size bed, neatly made with tight military corners. Without a word from his sealed lips, he unzipped it from the bottom and pulled out a dress. I didn't have to touch it to know the fabric had to be the most expensive silk with a lace overlay skirt that wrapped at the waist and flowed out. It was officially dated in terms of fashion trends, but I didn't care. It was beautiful.

It wasn't so much the dress that made the air in my chest grow shallow, but I sensed my dad was about to open up about something he'd never told me. He wasn't a man of many words, and most of his personal life was private. I remained respectfully quiet while he started his story with slow, carefully selected words.

"As you know, your mother and I never had a proper wedding. We said vows in the church rectory weeks before I got shipped to Iraq. Your mother had this dress but refused to wear it. She said it wasn't right for our little make-shift ceremony, and she wanted to save it for a big wedding. I'll never understand God's timing, but maybe he knew I'd need you. When I shipped out, we already knew you were on your way."

He sat on the edge of the bed, stretching his leg out as if his knee had been bothering him more than usual, and continued, "When I came home, I found this dress still hanging in the closet here, and I asked her to try it on. She *freaked* out, sobbing, so upset that I had seen it. I know what they say. How a groom wasn't supposed to see the dress, but we were already married with a baby. She refused to wear it until the 'big' wedding day, but she didn't want to set a date for our big wedding until she lost the baby weight. Such a perfectionist for details, but I didn't argue because I thought we'd have all the time in the world to make these memories . . ."

He lowered his gaze back to the dress, his lashes hooding his eyes perfectly so I couldn't see his inflections, but I heard a remorseful tone in his words. "No one tells you the things that hurt the most are the memories you didn't make. If I'd known then she would have a fatal seizure, I'd have made her wear the dress. Not just to the wedding, but at home, while we danced in front of the fire. Or shoot, I'd make her wear it to run through the rain, if I'd known that was her last chance." He raised his eyes to mine, and even though I'd expected them to be moist because mine were stinging, his were dry. It wasn't insensitivity, though. It was stoic. A deep line creased between his eyes, and he spoke in a stern voice, "Charlotte, life's too short *not* to wear the dress. Don't wait for perfection. Life is best lived pushing through the imperfections."

I swallowed hard, pushing down an entire flood of tears that threatened to tsunami down my face. I knew my mother had died from a seizure and that wasn't new. Throughout my entire life, I'd always wondered what moments would be like if my mother had been there. I never wanted for anything, but I always felt something was missing. This was the first time, I'd ever heard my dad speak of his loss. I'd never looked through his eyes and seen how hard that would have been for him, to do all the things with me, without Mom.

Although his story was a recollection of what he had lived, I knew it was purposely married with metaphors he wanted me to understand as life advice. He'd been nagging me for years to get married and have a family. I always assumed he didn't want me to be one of those old ladies who talked to vegetables. I saw his plight differently now. He'd been storing my mother's wedding dress all these years, and it had to be a haunting reminder of everything they put on hold for a better time, to eventually have no time left.

"What is anybody ever really waiting for?" His question hit me like a truck while his eyes pierced through the remaining layer of composure I had left.

His question had a haunting rhythm to it. I didn't want to waste my life waiting to make the memories, only to eventually run out of time. Reaching forward, I lightly grazed my fingers across the edge of the dress collar. It truly was the most beautiful dress I'd ever seen. Even though I didn't remember my mother, because I was a baby when she passed, I knew she would have been the most beautiful woman ever in this gown.

My dad's soft voice broke my thoughts. "I'm proud of you, Charlotte, for living your life. Promise me you'll wear the dress."

I ran my tongue along my lips, hoping it would make my words come out easier. Even though he was in control of his emotions, this conversation had caused my eyes to burn. I always thought my dad was a grump. I had no idea he was sentimental about this stuff. *I'm going to suffer dearly for these lies!* I blinked, securing the tears back as I mustered my reply, "I'll wear the dress."

Four
Charlotte

I closed the door to my Uber, and stared out the window, feeling more than a little apprehensive about this weekend. It was only a twenty-minute ride to the airport, so I had plenty of time to second, third and fourth guess myself. Before I drove myself nuts, I pulled out my phone and sought clarification one more time.

Me: I'm on my way. Are you going to be there?

Nick: I wouldn't be anywhere else. I have everything taken care of.

I reread his text twice, deciphering if there was double meaning in his words. They were vague and could mean a variety of things, but they also didn't rule anything out. They felt somewhat spontaneous and romantic. I bit down on my lip, suppressing a squeal as I couldn't believe I might actually be getting married. My mind walked through the steps that would have to happen if we were to get married.

Would he propose, or would it be a casual thing?

I wasn't what you call a hopeless romantic, especially this late in the dating game. I definitely saw myself having a traditional proposal, something I could look back on years later. If I was being honest, I also wanted a ring. I mean, the wedding only lasts an hour but the ring is what you had forever. I wouldn't be overly picky, though. I'd accept a ring from an arcade machine if it meant I could finally move to the next season of my life.

I blinked away my questions, letting the last one linger. *How would it feel to marry my best friend?*

It had to be the next best thing to finding a soulmate. Nick and I can talk about everything. It only made sense to marry him if I didn't want to end up alone. We already love doing everything together . . . Well, there are things Nick and I don't do. We don't kiss each other, but if we got married . . . My cheeks heated, and I quickly pushed *that* out of my mind. I couldn't think about that part. Especially since it was all just a joke.

"Phew." Letting out my breath, I heaved my rolling suit-case that wasn't exactly rolling because the left wheel had gotten jammed. It didn't help that the sidewalks were covered in dense snow, making it feel like I was off-roading a one-wheeled wagon. I dragged and shoved it—maybe kicked it once—through the entrance door of the Harbor Inn in Mapleton.

The lodge had a way of making me feel as if I was coming home for Christmas. It had perfect-Christmas splendor just like a movie set, complete with a large tree next to the stone fireplace and carols piping out the radio.

Out of the corner of my eye, I caught sight of a handsome man who looked like he could play the love interest in every Christmas romance movie—complete with scarf and matching sweater—smoothly wheeling in his two suitcases while his female partner casually strolled next to him without a hair out of place. She had one of those strides like she was walking a runway in slow motion. I tried not to ogle, but the jealousy was so thick it was seething right out of my mouth.

What I wouldn't do for a hunky man to tow my luggage around. I dropped a sigh that I would love to be able to describe as feminine, but at this point I had to admit it was on the spectrum closer to huffing.

"Oh, babe," I overheard the man say to his woman. "I'm going to help her. She's such a hot mess."

Maybe I should have been offended, but all I heard was the word hot.

He called me hot!

Doh, too bad he was taken.

The man parked his suitcases next to his partner and crossed the room, greeting me. "Hello, Miss. I can help you with that."

I didn't even pretend like I wanted to carry this cement brick of boulders by myself. Taking a grandiose side-step, I cleared his path to my suitcase, then cringed as he struggled to pull it forward.

"What on earth did you pack?" he grunted out.

"Err, just normal weddings stuff: a dress, toiletries, and a gallon of homemade Redeye." He gave me side eyes like I was a drunk, or something, so I tacked on, "It's a wedding tradition. My father's recipe. He didn't want me to be without it in case I get married this weekend."

"Oh," the woman exclaimed, slapping her cheeks with both palms. "Us too! It's been my dream to get married here since I was a little girl."

"You must be having a huge reception," the man added as he tugged on my suitcase until it was neatly parked next to the front desk. "That's a lot of shots to drink."

"Nah." I wagged my head, mulling over the oddities of our wedding arrangements. "It's not really a reception sort of thing. We are more like eloping, but my father couldn't fathom that a wedding would *not* need this much Redeye." I gnawed on my lip, knowing exactly how weird this looked. "I honestly don't drink but I didn't want to hurt his feelings." Then I rushed to change the subject,

"How about you? Are you having a large reception? I could totally donate some Redeye."

"Just one hundred of our closest friends and family," the woman explained, letting a Barbie smile fill her face. She reached out her hand, her French manicured tips were so perfect, I instantly got self-conscious of my home manicure. "I'm Alisa, by the way," she said. "And this is Jack."

"Oh," I took her hand, eagerly shaking it. "I'm Charlotte and my um, my Nick isn't here yet."

"Nick is your fiancé's name?" Alisa asked, with a tilt of her head in my direction.

"Ah, I'm not sure we did the whole fiancé thing?" I mused more to myself, trying to classify what Nick would be. "I think we skipped that step. He's more like my husband-on-hold sort of thing."

She gave me one of those looks that if she hadn't been so obviously pumped full of Botox would have made her brows bend down, but now she looked frozen.

"It's complicated." I waved a dismissive hand in her direction, wishing I could crack open the Redeye now. *This wasn't supposed to be this hard!* Suddenly, I was distracted by the sound of the door opening again, bringing in a massive gust of wind, a channel of shimmering snow, and Nick. My knees buckled, making me lean on the counter for a moment. *That's never happened before.* What an entrance that was! The glittering snow framed his way, making him look as if he was some movie star.

Our nervous eyes met, locking like they had so many times over the years, but yet everything was different. There were the expected specks of excitement he would get when he saw me after not seeing each other for a long time, but something else was there. Anticipation. Doubts?

"Here he is!" I exclaimed, gesturing toward Nick, who was now walking toward me. I honestly didn't think for a moment that the wedding thing would happen, but it was fun to joke about it. Like just for the weekend, I could walk around on his arm and introduce him as my future husband. It brought little butterflies to my gut, that I hadn't felt in years, and I'd be lying if I said it didn't make me feel slightly less lonely. I beamed back at my new friends and exclaimed, "This is my husband on hold."

Alisa and Jack laughed while Nick grinned at his new title, halting his steps a foot shy of me. Then he stood sort of wobbly as if he wasn't sure how to greet me. After swaying for a good ten seconds, he leaned in for a side hug. Hugging wasn't new for us—but it felt extra squeezy. I returned the affection by linking arms as we lined up to glance back at Jack and Alisa.

"So, Nick," I started, trying to bring him up to speed. "I was talking to this couple, and they are getting married this weekend."

"Oh, congrats." Nick nodded his head, taking his time to look at each of them individually.

"Yeah," Alisa started, "Charlotte told us you don't have a reception. That's a shame that you don't have anyone to celebrate with you."

"You know," Jack cut in, "You gave me a great idea. Our family isn't coming in until tomorrow. Why don't you two come to dinner with us tonight and we'll celebrate with you."

I trapped Nick's eyes, trying to read his thoughts, but he looked intrigued and gave me raised brows, so I assumed that was a yes. "I think that would be great," I answered for us both. "I mean, we don't have anything else to do tonight . . ."

Supercharged-to-gouge-my-eyes-out light pulled me from my slumber, but before I even opened my lids, I heard a faint snoring that whistled on the inhale, and vibrated rumbles on the way out.

Everything was light.

And not like celestial light, because I knew angels had trumpets, not nose horns.

Blinding light bore down on my irises, forcing me to wince as I shifted my gaze towards the piping snoring. Nick was sleeping on the chair next to the bed I was lying in. Even with my eyes still fighting to stay open, I couldn't miss him because his head was freshly shaved, and shining like it was recently waxed.

That's odd.

So odd.

Next to my dad, Nick was the most strait-laced guy I had ever met, and he never had a hair out of place. He wasn't the type of guy to shave his head. I studied his face, and realized that although he appeared fully asleep, the snoring was *not* coming from him.

I leaned up on my arm, trying to get a better view, but then something else I'd seen before caught my eye and panic grew in my chest as my eyes traced my arm all the way to my shoulder, and I stared down at my body.

I was wearing my mother's wedding dress!

Dad had insisted that I pack it "just in case." Maybe I secretly hoped I would need it, but the sight of me wearing it, without recollection of why, was freaking me out! Not like I'm scared but more like *I'm-gonna-ugly-cry* emotional.

I'd never even tried on a wedding dress in my life. Here I was wearing one, and not any random one, but my mother's! Dad told me to wear the dress, but *it wasn't supposed to be like this!* Fanning my face, fighting back the tears of emotion, as a distraction, I hyper-tuned to the mysterious snoring and forced myself to ignore the dress—*for now.* My eyes skirted to the side, dropping as the snoring seemed to come from the floor.

Like a spring was propelling it, my jaw plummeted, and I let out a scream of fright! *A giant Saint Bernard was sleeping on the floor!* It wasn't so much the sight of a dog lying next to me that scared me—although that was terrifying—but it was what this dog was wearing that made ice run through my veins. A perfect little dog bowtie with tiny but still clear-as-day letters printed on the back that read, "Best Man!"

"Nick," I whisper-screamed from across the room. "Nick, wake up. I think we got married!"

Five

Nick

I assumed it was another fantasy like all the others I had about Charlotte. Still consumed by a light haze of sleep, I could hear her sweet voice calling to me with melodic chords like adorable birds fluttering their wings while chirping out, "Nick" and "Married." My subconscious was teasing me—well more like tormenting me—pulling my mind to think of Charlotte and all that I wanted us to be.

Yet, as I came into consciousness, I noticed her sweet voice wasn't that melodic, but more like screaming with panic intonations like I was on fire, which frankly, scared me. My adrenaline surged, and I shot straight to my feet, ready to grab Charlotte and run to safety.

As my head exploded with pressure like an overinflated tire, I scanned the room.

A hotel room. Not just any hotel room, but one with a long trail of rose petals from the door to the bed . . .

Usually, when we met in Mapleton, I stayed with my folks while she stayed at the lodge, so I had to admit, it was a little odd we'd shared a room. I wasn't going to get totally hung up on that detail, though.

Across from me was a rather large cardboard Rudolph the Red-nosed Reindeer, which looked surprisingly like the one I had seen in the window of the general store the other day. That was weird, but still nothing to get hung up on.

Wincing over the rumble in my queasy gut, my eyes slid to Charlotte.

She was looking gorgeous in a *white* dress with so many ruffles it made me doubt it was an actual dress. It looked more like she was swimming in a cloud, but I didn't have the appropriate amount of time to dwell on that because what hooked my attention the most was she was growling at me.

A very realistic I'm-going-to-chew-your-face-off growl.

When did she learn to do that?

Something's out of place.

"Let's not panic." I took a timid step toward Charlotte as the growl dropped off into a snap. My gaze fell to the floor, and I jumped back a whole foot. There was a behemoth sized dog with a head so massive he could swallow me whole. Clearly, I was wrong about the growling coming from Charlotte, which made me feel so much better about Charlotte.

Okay, so there's a lot of misconceptions going on, even though things look a little strange. I'm sure there is a logical explanation for everything.

I inched forward, but the dog pulled back his thick lips into a snarl, revealing his giant fangs that would make a vampire jealous. "Nice doggie," I hummed out, hoping this dog was a vegetarian while still wondering the most obvious question, *where did Cujo come from!*

Apparently, he didn't like to be called nice, or something, because he snipped his puissant jaw forward, and growled ferociously. "That's a little dramatic. Don't you think?" I nervously rambled, while sliding my foot backwards. I was hyper-focused on his canine teeth. He had a severe overbite and desperately needed a doggie dentist as his teeth appeared unnaturally sharp.

"I saw a bag of treats." Charlotte's voice rang out, all cheery like we were at the zoo and this beast was caged behind a fence.

"I don't think he wants treats." I took another weak-kneed step back and avoided making eye contact with him. I didn't want him to accidentally think I was challenging him to a duel. "I think he wants *me.*"

Charlotte sprang off the other side of the bed and snatched a little pouch off the dresser. "Found them." She flashed the bag at me before rotating it to read. "It says, Christmas cookies for dogs. Oh, and look how cute they are." She held up one of the treats, identical to a Christmas cutout-cookie candy cane.

"I don't care if it looks like a turd." I slid my hand out sideways, wiggling my fingers for her to come nearer. "Just give it here." She dropped the bag in my palm. I didn't want to risk getting my hand bitten off by getting closer, so I tossed a cookie in an ungraceful Frisbee toss. Holding my breath, I watched him open his jaw like a giant hatch and swallowed it whole. His colossus eyes latched onto mine while he ran his tongue over those viper fangs. Squinting, I might have cowered a little as I waited for him to growl. Instead, he pushed his paws forward and reclined into a lying position, just as mellow as could be. "Maybe he was hangry," I whispered, still afraid to move.

"W-well, I mean," Charlotte's voice stuttered a little. "When's the last time he was fed?"

"Or how about the better question," I blurted out. "Who's dog is it? Where did he come from, why is he here, and—"

"That's three questions," Charlotte's voice came out with a humored inflection.

"You cut me off before I got to the best question of all," I went on without acknowledging her impressive math skills. "Why is he in a bowtie that says best man?"

"I was hoping you wouldn't bring that detail up."

"Why?" For the first time since hearing that furious growl, my eyes left the dog and hooked on Charlotte. "How can I not see that?"

"Um, I was hoping it was part of my over-active imagination, and thought if you didn't confirm it, I could pretend it wasn't like a *thing*."

"It's a *thing!*" My voice ticked up a notch, as I took an involuntary step, okay it was more of a stumble back. Now that I was not scared for my life, I rubbed my temples and prepared to address the next most obvious *thing* in the room. "Charlotte, you're in a wedding dress."

"It was my mother's," she said with a straight face.

"You knew about that?" I asked in an accusing tone, not because I was upset with her, but I was so confused.

"Well, sort of." Her head weighed to one side before she tacked on, "My Dad made me pack it, but I wasn't going to *wear* it."

"Charlotte," I said, my voice smooth and casual, but inside everything spun in all the wrong directions.

"Yes, Nick."

"I'm not certain about this." I swallowed the lump in my throat and plopped onto the corner chair, trying to remember what had happened last night but my mind was blank. Oh, Man! I wanted to marry Charlotte, had always wanted to marry her. But not like this! Not with all my memories wiped out, but I couldn't deny what had most likely happened. I continued, "But let's say it's at ninety percent and maybe a half-*ish*. I'm doing the math, but it's like the best man." I gestured to the dog. "Plus, wedding dress." I motioned to Charlotte. "Plus, honeymoon suite, and I don't remember anything, about anything. That all equals, in my head, I added it, and I-I think we got MAR-RIED!"

Six

Charlotte

"That's what I said!" I sputtered back at him, hoping to finally make sense of this mix-up. As startling as it was to wake up in my mother's dress, I was grateful I had clothes on. At least nothing *else* happened!

"You knew about this?" Nick's eyes—a hue so blue it twinned with the Adriatic Sea— sharply pierced into mine so hard it made my gut twist. Not in a dreamy way either, more like I felt it wise to pace to the side because he clearly looked like he was about to be ill.

"Um, maybe," I said softly. Insecurity filled my soul as I didn't enjoy seeing Nick upset at the thought of us being married. I hated it. "I mean, remember we talked about it. Right?"

"*Right.*" Nick paced forward, one eye on me and the other methodically sliding to the side, keeping tabs on the dog. "I don't remember anything. Do you? Do you know *for sure* what happened?"

Pulling my eyes away from his intense glare, I focused inward as I studied my memories. "The last thing I remember," I paused while I decoded the images in my mind. "I remember we went with our new friends and we all got that special poinsettia champagne. You know, the one with those adorable pine needles for a garnish. It was so cute. Oh, and it had a stick of cinnamon or something on it, too." I started to draw the length with my finger in the air. "It was brown and about this long. Do you remember that?"

"I remember the drinks—not with that much detail—but I remember making a toast and then clinking glasses with everyone and then . . . nothing."

"I don't remember the toast." My lips pursed out thoughtfully. "What was the toast?"

Nick's face dropped all color. The last time I had seen him that shade, was after he had gotten food poisoning from eating mystery chicken at a buffet. "We toasted to getting *married*."

Snorting sarcastically, like that *wasn't* the biggest clue to solving this conundrum, I rushed to stifle his words with new words of my own, "Okay, um there's a reason it looks this way but um, obviously we aren't seeing some clues."

"Right. This must be staged." He went to run a hand through his hair, the way he always did when he got overwhelmed, but when his hand met the buffed side of his head, he stiffened. "Charlotte," his voice rolled out smooth with obvious forced calm. "What is going on with my head?"

"It looks like you shaved it," I quickly replied, not wanting to waste time discussing hair. Hair wasn't as important as life-altering vows. My stomach had been tossed into a pit of quicksand, sinking lower with each new detail. I barely had time to think about hair.

He pivoted on his heel, rotating to face the mirror by the door. "I what?"

My eyes grew round, wondering how he could have missed what was happening with his own head. "You didn't know?"

He blinked so rapidly, I thought he'd sprain his eyelids. "You knew!"

I rushed behind him, meeting his gaze in the mirror. "It was one of the first things I noticed when I woke up."

His hands fled to the sides of his head, and he continued to rub it. "Why would I cut my hair?" He pressed his face to the mirror, turning his head in all directions, and ranted, "I have had the same hair cut for the last ten years. I get it trimmed at exactly every four weeks. I'm very precise about my hair. This should never have happened. Something is majorly wrong here!"

Lifting my shoulders, feeling lost hair was the least of my worries, I tossed out a reassuring, "It'll grow back."

Nick turned back to me, his face growing crimson, and his words were overly enunciated and broken. "What. Is. Going. On. Here?"

"Ah, let's go back to your theory about this being staged …" I didn't think anyone would stage something like this, but I wasn't ready to accept the most obvious explanation for this situation. It wasn't so much that I was upset that I might have gotten married to Nick, but more the thought that I didn't remember anything.

Tears welled in my eyes. I had been looking forward to my wedding since I was a little girl. I didn't always think I'd have a perfect day—though I dreamed of one—but I'd assumed I'd at least remember it. I paced down the little aisle next to the bed, away from Nick. "There must be a reasonable explanation for everything. Let's come up with a plan to retrace our steps. Maybe we can find people who remember seeing us, and they can tell us what happened?"

"Right?" Nick blew out a frustrated breath. I tilted my head, taking in the fact he was wearing a baby blue tux, like the kind you see in old movies. *That was odder than odd.* I didn't have time to bring it up, though because he rambled out an action plan, "The best place to start would be the chapel, right?" His eyes lightly treaded over my face. "I'm assuming if we got married, it would have been there."

I rubbed the side of my cheek, visualizing how this would all go down while still praying it was a bad dream. "Just walk right in and ask if we got married?"

"I've never been in this situation before, but if you have a better idea, now would be the time to voice it." He impatiently gestured to the dog, tacking on, "Because clearly, he knows what happened, but he isn't speaking."

I glanced at the dog, wanting to giggle, but I knew if I laughed, the amusement would quickly change to the fear that brewed inside me, and I'd start bawling. "No." I didn't want him to know I was feeling this way, so I quickly agreed. "Your idea is fine." My eyes caught my reflection in the mirror, and all I saw was white. I tried to forget the memory of my dad, telling me to wear the dress. He didn't mean to *waste* the dress on something so casual I can't remember putting it on. "I, ah, should change first," I muttered as I made my way to my suitcase and dragged it into the bathroom.

I shut the door with my flattened palm, and it wasn't until I felt the click of the door shutting, I noticed my fingers trembling. Sure, on the surface, one could chuckle about waking up in a wedding dress and having no memory, right? It was like a country western song. However, underneath the obvious jokes, I was left wondering how this would affect our friendship. There was clearly a broken boundary.

Marriage isn't a casual relationship.

I want to be married to someone I love. Sure, I love Nick but in a best friend kind of way. I'd never do anything to jeopardize that friendship. Joking about getting married had been so much more fun than waking up married. Since I don't remember what happened, I have no idea how I was even supposed to feel about this. How was I supposed to move forward?

As I tugged my dress over my head, I pushed the niggling thoughts to the back of my head.

Now, I was left holding my mother's wedding dress. Somewhere, in the time since my dad had given it to me, it had become a symbol of dreams not lived. This morning, as I clung to it and stared at my reflection in the bathroom mirror, I was now scared that everything had been pushed too far . . .

What happens when you force events that aren't meant to be?

I carefully hung up the dress, making sure it didn't snag and changed into casual clothes. As I returned from the bathroom, the dog rushed in front of me. Now he guarded the door, but wasn't unfriendly. His tail wagged and he bounced around, inviting himself to come with. "You can come." I smiled at him, and reached back, grabbing the bag of treats. "You might be ready for some real food anyway." I peered over at Nick. "Maybe we can grab some food on the way."

Nick slid his arms into his coat and took a moment to adjust the bottom, so it was straight. "Yeah, we can take my car, and stop at the general store." He motioned to the cardboard reindeer leaning against the closet door. "I remember seeing that in the general store display window, and it might not be a bad idea to see if anyone remembers us being there." Removing his keys from his pocket, he opened the door, waiting for me and the dog to walk through, and then tacked on, "Maybe we can grab a leash for him too. I'm not sure it's a good idea to just have him follow us?"

Never having owned a pet of any kind before, I raised my shoulder. "He made it here with us somehow?

"I know." Nick fell into stride with us down the hall, carrying the life-sized cardboard Rudolph in front of him. "We should ask around to see whose dog he is. Someone is probably missing him, and I don't want to be accused of dog napping."

I checked behind me, the dog trotted right in tow, with a happy face and dangling tongue. He didn't appear to be missing anyone. In fact, he didn't seem sad at all. The elevator door opened right as we made it to the end of the hall, and we entered, lining up with Rudolph between us. Once the door was closed, we stood so stiffly that you'd think we were strangers riding this thing together, and not best friends who might possibly be married. The elevator was slow as it ticked off floors on its descent. My eyes sprang wide when I absorbed Blue Christmas piping through the speakers. I didn't want to believe it might be an omen, but Nick blurted out the most random thing, "Do you believe in soulmates?"

Triple blinking, my face took a mild scowl. How dare he ask me that during *my* song! "Why would you ask that?" I choked out, feeling my throat instantly dry.

"It was a word fart," his voice was rushed, his body visually stiffened even more. "I didn't mean to."

I stared forward as the elevator ticked off another floor, and I surprised myself by replying, "I don't think so. I think the point of life is to find someone who can tolerate you, and then you drag each other to the finish line."

Even though I was dead serious, he let out a chuckle, "You don't really believe that, do you?"

"Yeah, I do." The elevator doors opened, and we stepped through them together, heading toward the parking lot. "I used to believe in soul mates when I was like nine years old, but now after having gone through my entire adult life being mostly single, while watching all of my friends get married, I have to think the concept is flawed. It doesn't make sense why some people find theirs so easily, while others must suffer through the dating pool for years." Tilting my head towards his thoughtfully, I added, "And not to mention those poor souls who never find their person. The whole idea is dependent on luck. Like what happens if you run to the bathroom at the exact moment you were supposed to spill hot coffee on your soulmate?" I shook my head like I was feeling shame. "So, yeah, I don't believe there is only one person for you. However, I do think it's possible to find someone you'd chase the stars for. But it's not luck. It's a choice."

Before, we were walking almost shoulder to shoulder, but it seemed as if he lengthened his stride, like he was trying to keep far away from me. *Maybe I hurt his feelings?* I didn't mean to, but I was massively overwhelmed about everything going on.

We were in the parking lot now, and Nick walked over to a late nineties style two-door lowrider Honda and waited for me, obviously avoiding my gaze. "This is your car?" I asked, feeling a little confused. For a man who was always impeccably dressed in office wear, I was expecting something not so . . . punk high school. "I thought you were rich," I teased.

His lips pinned an even smile on his face, revealing his perfect teeth. I could tell it was fake because when he genuinely smiled his teeth parted and now, they were clenched. Now I was mostly sure I had hurt his feelings, but I couldn't deal with anything more than what was at hand. I didn't want to be insensitive, but I also couldn't risk any more emotions as I could feel tears still weighing on the back of my eyes. "You are the one who always said I was rich," Nick replied. "This was my high school car. My parents saved it because my dad drives it to work to save on gas, but yeah, since I flew here, I just drive this around."

I stared at the rusted-out wheel wells, and my gaze traced the bubbled paint. "How come I never noticed it before?"

It was a simple question, that barely touched on what I wanted to ask. I was actually massively curious now about what else I'd missed. And how?

"We usually just walk around downtown." He tossed a shoulder up, and climbed inside his door, calling back, "Hold up a second before you try to open your door, I have to unbuckle it."

"Don't you mean unlock it?" I wasn't sure why I corrected him; I knew what he meant, but then I didn't . . . He moved his seat forward, letting the dog jump in the back seat, taking a moment to secure Rudolph in the backseat as well. Then he leaned over the middle console, unlatched the seat belt wrapped around the door handle and gave a nice hard shove. "Hop in," he called.

Everything about this car felt illegal, and like I should be strapping on a helmet, and combat boots. I found myself glancing over my shoulder before I slid in and slammed the door, but I wasn't surprised when it didn't latch. A smirk brewed on my lips, and I tried hard to bite it back. Even though I teased Nick about being rich because he lived in New York, I knew Nick's family was working class—and this car or any car they had—was something they worked hard for. I looked at Nick, a sarcastic grin laced his lips as he held up the seat belt for me in the most telling way. I couldn't help it, and I burst out laughing. "You are telling me I have to latch the door closed with my seat belt?"

Scowling, he wasn't even trying to fake a smile. "The door stopped sticking years ago," his voice was apologetic. "Dad never thought it was worth it to spend the money to fix it when he had this trick. I can latch it for you, if you want, but yeah, I don't want you to fall out of the car."

"Such a gentleman," I joked, but his lips never quivered into a smile. We'd always joke about everything, and the fact that he didn't at least smile, made me think I'd upset him. He had a good sense of humor though, so maybe it was something else? Maybe he was upset we got married?

I sandwiched my back against the seat, motioning for him to lean over me. And he was a gentleman when he threaded the belt through the door handle, and snapped it into place. When he reached over to give it a test yank, I couldn't help but let another rush of laughter fall out of my mouth. "No wonder you get all the ladies. I can't believe I've been missing out."

"Right?" he easily made fun of himself, but didn't stop testing the belt as he pushed on the door, testing it. "You'll be okay." He didn't even try to pass a tiny glance in my direction, and at this point, I knew he was sad.

He cranked the engine, backing up swiftly while a weird ticking noise came from the floorboards. I pretended to ignore it. He shifted the car into drive and then out of what seemed like nowhere, he said, "I don't think you choose."

"Huh?" My eyes slid over, meeting his briefly before he turned his attention back on the road. "What are you talking about?"

"Soulmates," he stated firmly. "I don't think it's as easy as picking someone, or them picking you." He rested one hand on top of the wheel and leaned back, relaxing in the seat.

Or maybe the seat is just broken and he had to lean like that?

"I think," Nick continued, "sometimes you meet someone—that person who just fits perfectly and you can't imagine your life without them." His words came out laced with spite, as if he was furious about someone who had jilted him. I have no idea what woman he'd be upset about, because he hadn't mentioned anyone he was dating, or getting deeply hurt.

"Wow." I mulled over his very thoughtful response. "That's deep thinking." I stole a look at him, noting although he always had a great head of hair, he looked extremely handsome with a shaved head. It gave him an edge. I didn't hate his new haircut.

His comment about soulmates made me think about my parents, and I felt like I needed to explain the random wedding attire from this morning, "You know," I started, still holding my gaze on him. "My mom had bought that wedding dress, and never wore it because she was waiting until the perfect 'big' wedding, but she never had a chance before she died." I paused, running my tongue along my lower lip, not really sad, but mostly wanting to take a moment to give Nick a chance to digest what I was saying. Although my life was an open book to him, my mom wasn't someone I had talked about much. "My dad had made me promise to stop waiting for the perfect moments in life. His exact words were that the things that hurt the most are the memories my parents never made." I waved a flippant hand, adding in an equally dismissive tone, "That's why I had the dress. He made me promise to wear it."

Nick raised his chin slowly, nodding until his words floated out softly. "Carpe diem."

"Huh?" I had barely heard his whisper and leaned toward him, hoping to hear better.

"You know the saying, seize the day. Live each day to the fullest." He pulled into a parking space in the alley behind Mapleton General Store and threw his car into park. "I love what your dad was saying. It is the perfect outlook." Without missing a beat, he jumped out of the car, pushed his seat forward, letting out the dog, and grabbed Rudolph. "Are you ready?" he called back from his place on the street.

I struggled to thread the seatbelt back through the door handle, so it didn't get further tangled. I wasn't trying to be a jerk, but I couldn't help but sputter out a laugh as I replied, "I need a minute to unbuckle. This is a new thing for me."

"Let me do it." He sat back down on the driver's seat, leaned across me, and reached for the belt. "I wrap it four times to use all the slack, so it doesn't come loose."

"I didn't know there was a trick." I straightened my spine, trying to flatten out against the seat while he practically laid his body in my lap as he unwrapped the belted door. Not sure why that sent a thrill through my body. It was a bit odd. His face was so close to mine, I could smell his breath. I'd known Nick for years, and we'd done many weird things together, but we'd never been in this position before. Luckily, he was an expert in unlatching a seat-belted door and he quickly opened my door, and finally sat up straight.

I bit back a giggle, as this seemed like it was so much extra work. "I can crawl through your door next time."

He offered me a fake smile as I slammed my door as hard as I could and then patiently waited for him to latch the door back. By the time he joined me on the curb, the dog was back to doing his hangry howl. "Oh." I pushed my hands into my bag, pulling out the candy cane treats. "I know what you want." I gave him a smile and tossed him the candy cane that he caught midair. He swallowed it whole and ceased the howling, so maybe I had read his cues correctly.

"Nice doggie." I patted his head with a super straight arm, trying to keep as much distance between us as possible. I wasn't afraid of dogs, but I never had the chance to warm up to them. I wasn't well versed in their language. The whole howling, slobbering thing was a tad off-putting. Now that he was happy, he bounced around, as if he had a tap dance he couldn't hold in, I found him quite entertaining. Frankly, he was the distraction I needed, but even with this adorable dance, I couldn't help but bite the inside of my cheek.

"All right?" With Rudolph tucked under one arm, Nick stepped forward, opening the store door for me. "We're here," he added, after the decorative strand of old-fashioned jingle bells were done ringing. "Let's see if we can solve this enigma."

Seven

Charlotte

"We could start by finding some food for our best man." I wandered down the narrow aisle that was completely bare on both sides. In college I'd spent some time working in retail and I knew the first aisle was always the most important to merchandise. It was odd that the storekeepers had failed to fill it with anything. I kept walking until I rounded to the next aisle. Everything was so crammed. I literally halted on my heel, the dog crashed into the back of my leg, but I barely noticed because I was scratching my head.

Why is this aisle so cluttered, but they had an empty aisle next to it?

Surely, they could spread out their stuff a little more. Shaking my head, I contemplated how small towns are peculiar sometimes. I continued to pace through the aisle, finding it seemed to hold a little of everything as most small-town general stores did. "Do they have stuff for animals here?"

"I'm sure they have a shelf somewhere." Nick butted up behind me with a tiny shopping cart that reminded me of one of those child's play ones. He had managed to stuff Rudolph into it, or well, he got the first two legs in the cart and then balanced the rest of it on top. I let out a small chuckle because it was one of those things that happened whenever I hung out with Nick. We could do the most mundane and boring things, like shop for dog food, and he always found a way to make me laugh.

His gaze scanned the bottom shelf with the largest bags and boxes of items. "I see birdseed down there." He motioned to the very end of the aisle. "I'm guessing the dog food would be next to it." He was already on it, and scooped up a huge sack and placed it in the bottom of the cart. "Got the dog food." With the giant Rudolph still protruding out, the stuffed cart proved challenging for Nick to maneuver around the displays. "Now let's see if we need to return this Rudolph."

A lady stood behind the checkout stand, and I hadn't thought about how awkward this would be to ask if we had stolen something. I mean, I'm sure we didn't actually *steal* it, but I couldn't imagine another reason for us having guardianship of the missing Rudolph. I waited until she looked up and then pointed to Rudolph. I wondered what she already knew but I held onto a squeamish smile, hoping she was nice.

"I, or we, found this and we're pretty sure it belongs here." I motioned to the front store window display, which had a near-life-sized Santa's sleigh with six reindeer lined up. A spot in the front of the pack was open and obviously missing a deer.

She remained quiet, and stepped closer to the window, eyeing the display. At this point, I wish I hadn't said anything. We should have just dropped the deer off and run. *Is she going to call the cops over something so stupid?* This having to explain stuff was going to be tough. I glanced at Nick and he seemed to be thinking the same thing as he shimmied a little closer to the door. We took a step in unison but froze when we heard clapping rise up from behind us.

Even before I turned around, I could feel the noise directed at us. Nick pivoted first. His eyebrows quivered slightly, before fixing into a bent-down angle. I turned, my eyes were met with four people standing in a row, all clapping with giant smiles on their faces as if not only did they know us, but we had done the most amazing thing ever. They were wearing matching red vests, as they clearly employees, but that didn't explain why they acted this way.

I flicked my hand up into a nonmoving wave, hoping to make the noise stop, but instead they cheered harder with one lady on the end calling out, "We love you!" She grabbed Nick's hand and squeezed it so hard, it made Nick's eyes nearly bug out of his head. *What did we do?*

That was strange. Surely, they had us mistaken for someone else, a celebrity, maybe? I mean, I get told all the time I look like a young Anne Hathaway. Feeling a little flattered, I ran a hand along my dark hair, smoothing it out, and smiled as sweetly as possible while flashing my best side at them. "Hello."

They finally pulled the plug on the clapping, and the lady at the end stepped toward us. She pushed her shoulders back and locked eyes with me. "My staff told me about what you did yesterday, and I can't express myself enough to say thank you. It's truly a Christmas miracle."

Pushing my thumb against my chest, I stuttered, "Uh m-me?"

She raised her hands out to us and exclaimed in a jubilant voice, "Both of you, of course."

My eyes slid to Nick's, hoping he had an inkling of what was going on, but the shrug he gave me told me he was equally as confused. "R-right." I stuttered through gritted teeth. "What we did. Ha-ha." A wave of terror crashed over me, crushing. Suffocating. I completely regretted even getting out of bed this morning. I should have just skipped today. Nothing was going well. I don't remember seeing any of these ladies, let alone setting foot inside this building. "This is totally strange." I continued to smile while I nudged the lady with a friendly elbow. "Say, um, do you mind telling *us* what we did?"

Her lashes fluttered but she stayed mute as she stared back at me, and I tacked on, "We sort of can't remember yesterday." Wincing, I looked at Nick to rescue me.

He stepped forward while adding, "We're missing a few hours, but we had Rudolph, so we thought we'd start here. We were hoping someone could tell us what happened."

"Oh!" Her eyes rounded, while they continued to shine on Nick and me. "I could tell you, but it would be easier to show you." Spinning on her heel, she hustled into the empty aisle, spreading her arms open wide in motion to the shelves. "Our store sponsors a Giving Tree for kids who don't have toys for Christmas. During the month of December, we stock toys, and collect donations from customers. This year's donations were drastically lower than expected. You guys walked in the door right as the town Santa came to retrieve the toys, and it startled you, seeing Santa. You accidentally knocked the tree over. Santa helped you put the tree back together, but when you saw so many kids who needed toys, you bought and donated *all* the toys to Toys for Tots. You cleaned us out." Her smile was giddy when she added, "We were so grateful for the donation, we gave you each a candy cane, and that Rudolph as a gift."

"A toy drive?" Then again small towns were so wholesome to do something like that. That was an extremely nice gesture from us, and I could see why they were happy to see us again because we had to have spent a fortune—"Wait a second," my voice rushed out, as my chest filled with terror. "What do you mean, we *bought* all the toys?" My throat flexed, tightening even more, and I barely squeaked out. "How did we buy them?"

My eyes met Nick's, and we had a moment where I knew we were thinking the same thing. It was evident by the flaming hue of red which washed over his ears. His ears had always served as a barometer for his emotions, and I never had to ask what he felt. He was flashing that red-hot thing that happens when he's holding in all of what is getting ready to explode out.

The lady stepped toward the till, speaking in a voice a little louder than a mutter. "Well, I can double check if you need to know card numbers, but you both had a few credit cards which we used to split it all up."

"A few?" My jaw dropped as my eyes immediately pulled back to the *empty* aisle and I started to do math. *How many toys did we buy!*

"Oh yes," she went on as she tugged back the lid on the old-fashioned receipt printer and pulled out the yellow receipt log. "We maxed out the first card with just the first load."

The knot in my throat swelled at an alarming rate. So much so, I figured it would suffocate me in a second. The good news was I wouldn't have to worry about credit card bills. Since I was suffocating, I figured nothing worse could come from getting more clarification. "So, do you remember how much the total bill was?"

"Oh yes." She nodded, still smiling as if she thought this was the most exciting thing to ever happen. "It was seven thousand, three hundred dollars—"

"Oomph!" I called out, grabbing my stomach, fighting hard not to faint. My feet involuntarily flopped in a circular pattern as if I had sprouted flippers with no training wheels. Clearly, I had lost my ability to balance.

"I just threw up in my mouth." Nick proclaimed as one hand flew over his mouth. His other hand clambered to the nearest counter as if he was also suffering from the inability to stand. He steadied himself by leaning on the counter but raised his face to the woman. "I drive a Honda. Where on earth did we put all these toys?"

She waved her hand in a dismissive way. "We loaded them in Santa's sleigh, and he was off to deliver them."

Nick's gaze slammed to mine, a look of determination budding in his eyes as he declared through deep measure breaths, "We must find that Santa!"

I nodded because making a sound wasn't possible. At this point, I felt like a windstorm had blown me over, and I dropped my head between my knees as I struggled to breathe.

Now that my head was between my legs, I could see the dog who had apparently been behind me this whole time, tongue hanging out as if he was as happy as can be.

At least someone was still happy.

Eight

Nick

"This is so much worse than getting married," Charlotte huffed out, as she climbed over the driver's seat in my Honda, shimmying to the passenger side while trying to not get hung up on the handbrake. "I don't have money to blow on kids I don't know."

I wasn't happy about the unexpected expense but in retrospect it could have been worse. At least it was only money. I was more upset about Charlotte getting so stressed out. It still felt surreal that I wasn't able to remember anything about last night. I'm usually always the responsible guy, and I can't believe I let all this happen.

"It's Zemblanity." My voice was low while I waited for the dog to climb into the back seat. He seemed used to us by now, obeying me when I asked him to do things. He was turning out to be an easy keeper, even if he didn't take his eyes off the giant bag of dog food that I sat in the seat next to him.

Charlotte peered over her shoulder. "Zemblian—what?"

"It's the opposite of serendipity. Instead of a happy accident, it's a bad discovery."

"It's exactly what you said. It's super Zemblian." Charlotte fretted while dropping her head into her palms, burying her face. Her words muffled as she continued, "I can't afford to spend that kind of money on anything. What are we going to do?"

As much as I wasn't ecstatic about the money, I just wanted to make Charlotte happy again. "It'll be okay." I slid into my seat, pulled the door closed, and placed my arm on her shoulder. "We still have no idea if she was telling the truth. We can call our card companies to verify. Maybe she was wrong?"

"I saw the receipt." Her voice was pitching louder now, and she was starting to wail. "We are stuck paying for this!"

I hated seeing Charlotte this upset. Feeling this failure deep in my gut, I gently squeezed her forearm, forcing a calm tone even though I felt the panic plucking away at my voice. "It'll work out. It's not even Christmas. I'm sure the town Santa hasn't delivered the presents yet, and he is stockpiling them. We can find him and negotiate something. Maybe we can take most of the toys back in exchange for helping him hand them out. If we explain everything, he'll see it was a huge misunderstanding."

Charlotte's words were barely audible as she sobbed into her hands. I couldn't comprehend a single word, but it tugged at my heart. I felt entirely responsible. I should have protected her more, and we wouldn't have all this confusion and heartbreak. My brain was still so clouded, and as hard as I tried to remember what had happened, I had a void in my memory with no real solution on how to get my memory back. Evidently, asking around town was making everything worse.

This weekend was not turning out the way I had hoped. I had planned a whole romantic weekend, full of all the Christmas card-cute activities, hoping Charlotte would finally see me as more than a friend. Now, I'd ruined her whole life. I didn't have the money to pay for the toys any more than she did, but she looked so hopeless as she sobbed into her hands. I reached my arm all the way around her shoulders and pulled her into a hug. "It's okay. I'll pay for all the toys."

"You can't pay for them all," she sniffed into my shirt, "it's too expensive."

"Nah, I can write it off as a donation under my business expenses," I downplayed the offer, but I really had no clue if I could do that or not. I didn't want her to worry. Then in the most honest voice I could muster up, I tacked on, "I'm sure it was my idea more than it was yours."

"It doesn't matter." She lifted her face and swiped at her nose. Her being this close to me, with this much vulnerability was having a strange effect on my heart rate, making me feel like I was doing some vigorous activity, instead of just sitting here holding my breath. I got scared to talk, afraid I'd say the wrong thing. Only inches from her, I stared into her bright green eyes, feeling a zing of something spicy rocket right to my heart. It wasn't new. I chalked it up to all the stupid ways my body reacted when I was near Charlotte. I pretended not to notice the mascara streaks she left on my good shirt. Oddly, it made me feel good that I could be the one to hold her this close and end up with her mascara stains. Even if I was still in the friend zone.

"It was obviously both of us who bought them, so we should take responsibility together." She dabbed both of her eyes, and spoke softly as if she was talking more to herself. "I'll have to see if I can get a waitress job, or something on the weekend, and I can pay the bill off faster."

Finally, her tears stopped cascading, and she held her gaze steady as if she were deep in thought. Her face was still only inches from mine, and I was mesmerized by her. Her beauty was so striking, it was like time stood still. For me, anyway. The world around us faded, and all I saw was her gorgeous face staring back at me. Until she broke my daydream. "Where to now? We returned Rudolph. Do we want to continue to the chapel or track down this Santa guy?"

"Oh, right." I returned my mind to the present. "Well, although we both want to find out our marital status, I feel like the Santa guy is the more urgent issue at hand because if we catch him before he hands out all the toys, we may be able to get most of our money back. What do you think?"

"Agreed." Her words rushed, hinting she was still distraught about the money. She nodded behind me. "Maybe we should feed the dog before he gets hangry."

"Yeah, um." I considered the best way to do so. I didn't have anything that could serve as a bowl, and I wasn't sure why I didn't think to buy one. *Oh wait, I remember why! It was the shock of learning I was bankrupt!* "Okay." I let out a defeated sigh before opening my door again. Let's walk down to the Christmas tree. We can make a little picnic for him." A picnic for a dog sounded stupid, and I knew that, but I was so overwhelmed I didn't have the mental space to care. I offered my hand to Charlotte when she got of the car, and the moment our fingers touched, I felt another zap in my heart. This time I blamed it on static electricity, and not the fact that I had been in love with her for years.

Denial would be my new defense.

With Charlotte back on the curb, I pushed the seat forward again, and reached for the dog food, realizing yet another thing I had forgotten at the store. "I knew there was a reason I didn't have a pet, because clearly, I'm terrible at this." I gave Charlotte an even stare and then tacked on, "We forgot a leash."

She hiked a thumb over her shoulder back at the building. "Do you want me to run back in to grab one?"

"No," I spit out firmly. "We can never go back there again." My voice took a humored inflection. "The damage is too deep, and we must forever cut ties."

She busted out laughing. I'm sure the stress had been mounting, and this was the tip of it, but seeing her smile and laugh made me finally feel at ease and I joined in, laughing until we both had tears in her eyes.

Charlotte's lips were still curled when she finally managed to speak, "you have always had a flair for the dramatic."

I didn't have a leash, or dog skills, so I did what felt natural and patted my leg while making eye contact with the dog, "Here, Buddy." Like a magic trick in a perfectly rehearsed show, he came right to me. At least one thing was working out in our favor today. Leaning back into the car one last time, I grabbed the dog food and motioned to the gazebo. "This way, Buddy." I whistled, and he followed me again. Tearing off the top of the bag, I figured there was no harm in letting him eat right out of it. I set it on the ground, and he didn't waste a moment burying his head into the pebbles, chomping away.

Inhaling the fresh air and scent of pine pitch, I took a moment to take in the nativity scene set up in the gazebo. A typical manger and shepherd thing was going on, but a few odd things stuck out. One: all the shepherds and animals wore Santa hats with price tags still attached. That was super odd . . . I stepped closer and spotted a small teddy bear in the crib with baby Jesus. Pursing my lips, I picked up the bear and turned it over in my hand. Mapleton General Store price tag was still intact. Odder. I looked back at the crib where the bear had been and found a card.

Okay . . . someone left baby Jesus a note. That's cute.

Alright, I'm nosey. I picked up the note, unfolding it. Handwriting looked familiar. It looked a lot like Charlotte's loopy letters. She was the only person who put loops on both ends of her capital Cs. It's how she signed her name but carried that detail through to the rest of her writing. Oddest. I did a fast eye sweep, checking on Charlotte. She had plopped down next to the dog and seemed to enjoy watching him eat. I quickly turned my back so she couldn't see the letter and I read on.

All I want for Christmas is to find my husband. And if you can't do that this year, can you at least send a sign that I shouldn't give up. A shooting star or

The note was ripped off mid-sentence, with the bottom half completely missing. It didn't have a signature, but I had no doubt this was Charlotte's writing. We clearly had hit up this gazebo on our run last night. I quickly stuffed the note in my coat pocket, feeling my fingers bud up against the box I had been hiding while wishing Charlotte had wished for *me*. A deep yearning in my gut culminated into what felt like a sickness, niggling me that Charlotte would probably *never* wish for me. Some people would call it heartbreak, but it was more profound than that.

It was a serious case of *Sehnsucht*. That deep, sad yearning that makes you ill.

Nine

Charlotte

I didn't even bounce when I face splashed. So much for walking on the ice-frosted gazebo in heeled boots. It was above seasonal average temperatures, and the ice was melting, already accumulating a nice layer of water on top, making it slick. Lying on my stomach, the icy top layer of water seeped through my thin jacket, and my mind was screaming at me to get off the flipping ground! However my eyes were stuck on the barber pole down the block.

"Are you okay?" Nick hustled over, taking a knee next to me, so quick to wrap his strong arms around me, pulling me to my feet before I had time to get wetter. I held onto him even after I had found my footings, and a strange sensation washed through me. My body fit perfectly into a little Nick nook created by his hold on me. A perfect snuggery. A shudder shot through me. I had to resist resting my head against him and snuggling.

That would be weird.

We definitely didn't do stuff like that!

No sir!

Instead, I straightened my back, and took a small step out of the embrace. "I'm fine," I said, mostly to reassure myself. Wiggling my limbs, I did a mental inventory of my extremities to ensure everything was still functioning. Pleased with my findings, I took a deep breath and changed the subject. "So, the dog is fed. Still no sign of Santa, but I did notice a barber shop pole on the other side of this gazebo. Do you suppose that's where you had your head shaved?"

He placed his palm on the side of his head and ran it down the back, hooking it on his neck as if checking for at least one patch left of hair. "It would have to be because I didn't bring a clippers or anything that could get it this smooth and that's the only place in town." His eyes focused on the pole before he voiced what I had been thinking, "Maybe we should walk over there and see if they remember us?"

I was already pacing a step ahead of him up the street. It was like the dog had already become enmeshed in our little family, too, because we didn't even have to ask him. He skirted along on our heels, happily letting his tongue hang out. My hip throbbed from where I had landed on it, but it wasn't anything I couldn't ignore. At this point, it definitely was the least of my worries. With a mystery wedding, a maxed-out credit card, and a homeless dog all being at the top of my urgent fix-it list.

I shivered as I was chilly but not to the point past comfortable. In fact, if I hadn't gotten damp from tobogganing on my belly, I don't think I'd feel overly cold at all. The early afternoon air had notes of pine and hinted at forthcoming snowflakes. We passed the Main Street businesses, all decorated for Christmas, but with Mapleton it was more than just Christmas décor that created the ambiance. It was like this town was built for a Christmas postcard, with each building so quaint and perfect. It's one of the many reasons I loved coming here this time of year. You'd have to be a real Scrooge not to feel the Christmas spirit in the air. Corny, yes, but even with the recent streak of bad luck and now my bum hip, there was something about this little town at Christmas. It made me think that anything was possible.

"Are you sure you're okay?" Nick's low voice broke my concentration.

"Yeah. Totally." I shrugged off his concern while continuing to stride forward.

"You're walking with a bit of a limp." Tilting his head a measure closer to me, he added, "Let me help you."

"I'm fine," I tried to breeze over his comment. "Nothing walking won't stretch out—" My voice dropped off as Nick hooked his arm into mine. Tightly. Goosebumps trickled down my arm, in a way that had never happened before when I looked up at him. His dark eyes were wide with obvious concern, and a single worried line pinned on top of his nose.

"You're not going to take no for an answer," my voice came out in a whisper because something about being this close to Nick, under the downtown Christmas lights, stole the breath from my chest.

"It's not about taking no for an answer. I want to make sure you're okay, because I care about you." His cadence was slower than usual, hanging in the air. I knew he cared about me. We'd been friends for years, texting almost daily and meeting yearly when our schedules allowed. It wasn't that he said he cared that made my toes curl under. It was everything about the careful manner with which he spoke those words that made me think there was perhaps, a double meaning.

Or maybe I was hoping? Which is completely silly. He undoubtedly was making sure I hadn't busted my leg and nothing more.

Because why would it be more?

This stupid marriage pact has gotten my brain so garbled up.

"You're shivering." His brows bent down, and he immediately shook off his coat, saying, "Your jacket is soaked, and you should remove it. You can wear mine until your coat dries."

I started to decline, but stopped because I wanted his coat. It looked heavier than mine, and it was at least dry. Plus, having someone want to take care of me felt good. Smiling sweetly, I slipped off my own jacket and accepted his. A layer of warmth covered me, and I immediately felt right at home in it, even with the scent of his musky aftershave permeating the air. Actually, the musky man smell was rather amazing. It put an extra pep in my step, as I flung my old coat over my arm and carried on.

We arrived at the barber shop, and Nick pulled the heavy door open for me, and we both entered the building.

It was a typical barber shop setting with a couple of barber chairs, a table of magazines by the waiting chairs, and a shelf of retail products. There was a cute Charlie Brown Christmas tree perched in the center of the large window that made me smile, especially when paired with the Bing Crosby Christmas carols piping out.

A lanky man with his silver hair slicked back and a mistletoe bowtie stood watching the only TV on the wall. I didn't even have to ask if he recognized us, because his greeting said it all. "Mr. and Mrs. Cane. It's nice to see you again."

Everything about that sentence was wrong!

First off, Cane wasn't either of our surnames, so where in the mistletoe mania did he come up with that? I instantly got dizzy. It was getting to be too much to learn. However, as much as that detail made my brain swell, the thing my brain latched onto was the Mr. and Mrs. because, well, why wouldn't that be a problem? I mean, Nick and I were friends. We weren't supposed to be connected by those cute, little titles of companionship because, well, that would be wrong! Right?

My gaze slammed to Nick, hoping he could talk our way out of this one, but one look at him told me he was as flustered as I was. Despite the chill in the air walking down here, he now had a shimmering drop of perspiration bead on his brow. "Nick." I elbowed him, still hoping he could be the saner one in this situation. "Why are you sweating?"

"I'm not sw-sweating," he stammered. "It's a slight issue of my accismus not working." I had no idea what that meant, but I didn't dare ask because he looked like he was suffering. His chest rose slowly, but his deep breaths didn't calm him. His voice held a squeak when he added, "I knew I was a mister, but the whole other word sort of threw me off." He took a wobbly step toward the barber chair. "Phew, normally I can fake being calm, but that mode is so broken right now." His breath blew out loudly, and he gripped the armrest with one hand while he helped himself to the seat before the barber had a chance to invite him. "I'm going to sit here if you don't mind." He finally stared the barber straight in the face. "I need to ah, catch my bride—I mean breath."

As much as I was similarly shocked by the prefixes, see-ing Nick react this way made me giggle. Having outside confirmation of those titles was enough to shock us both. I stared at the floor, the checkered linoleum seemed to wave, as if it was threatening to open and suck me into the deep abyss. Clearly, I was dizzy too, and I grabbed the wall to steady myself. I finally looked back at the barber, "So, you do know us?"

His thin lips slid into an easy grin, and he chuckled. "How can I forget you two?"

"It's interesting that you say that," Nick cut in, his voice high-pitched and rushed, "because well, we don't remember you." With wide eyes and brows pulled high, Nick peered at the barber, and began to plead with his hands folded in prayer at his chest. "I don't remember anything! I'm sorry to lose my mind in front of you like this but when did I change my last name to Cane?"

Thankfully, the barber must have had a sense of humor because he didn't seem put off by Nick's breakdown. Instead, he grabbed a washcloth from the cupboard, and rinsed it under the tap. He folded it into a perfect rectangle and walked over to Nick, placing it on his forehead. "Relax," he said, in a soothing voice. "We have lots of grooms freak out like this. I'm used to it." As he turned his back, striding away from Nick, he muttered under his breath, "Of course, it's usually before the wedding, but nothing surprises me anymore."

"Groom?" Nick had clearly found his voice now, getting over the squeaky pre-pubescent boy thing he had going on earlier. Now he was letting out a full-blown wail. "Why can't I remember this!"

"I may be wrong about this," the barber started, "but I think you had a bit of a daze going when I saw you both."

"Knock me over with a feather boa." Nick's fake surprised voice rang out. "Of course, we did! I can't understand why, because all we had was one sip of a drink from the Lodge."

The barber's chin inclined, and he calmly rubbed his neck. "Poinsettia champagne?"

Nick's face froze. "How'd you know?"

The barber tossed up one shoulder in a shrug, but his expression said he wasn't confused at all. He had a tight, knowing smile sealing his lips. If I didn't know better, I would have guessed he was holding back a secret. "It happens every year around this time." The barber glanced over at me, a twinkle sparkled in his eye. "I've heard the rumors my whole life. For years, I thought it was a legend, but once I opened this shop, I started to see some of the couples. Some people blame the town. Some people blame the season. Some people say it's the champagne." His smile grew wistfully. "Call me a romantic, but I think it's fate."

"What's fate?" Nick and I blurted simultaneously, both of our gazes firmly locked on the barber.

His smile stayed strong, but his gaze flicked from Nick back to me. "I call it the Holidaze. You come here to Mapleton for a vacation, perhaps? Or maybe for work.

Some people have lived their entire lives here, but for some unsuspecting singletons, they live through a series of events—some of them a little crazy—and end up together."

"So, you know about this?" Nick sat up straighter in the chair, perching on the edge. "How do we find out what happened?"

The barber moved to his vanity, picked up a small dusting brush, and swiped it around the edges of his counter. Keeping his head down, he spoke matter-of-factly. "I can tell you what I know."

Nick grabbed both armrests, and set his jaw. "What happened?"

"On Fridays, I shut the doors later than usual. With it being payday for most people, I tend to be busy all day, and last night was no exception. I worked steadily until after nine, and I was locking up when you two came running up, knocking on my door." He raised his eyes to acknowledge Nick. "You, Sir, had a candy cane stuck in your hair, and it was such a mess, you couldn't get it out. I was teasing you, calling you Mr. Cane. I let you in and we shaved everything off, but you managed to save part of candy cane." The barber started chuckling through his words as he went on, "You held it out, not really paying attention to what you were doing, and that dog," he motioned to our new buddy. "ran right over, took a giant lick of it, and stayed glued to your side."

"You know this dog?" Nick waved toward our little friend. "Where did he come from?"

The barber gave a couple of even nods. "He's mostly from the streets. He's been coming around for the last couple of weeks, and sometimes when it's cold out, I let him in to warm up. My clients enjoy seeing him here. That's what happened last night. My client had let him in, and I had yet to turn him out. So, when he tried to go home with you, and you didn't stop him, I just waved him on. He instantly attached to you."

I looked back at Nick, feeling a tinge of relief. "At least we know we didn't rob a pet store or something stupid."

"Right," Nick agreed, but his voice still held a worried inflection. "So, what else happened? Did we say where we got the candy cane?"

The barber pushed his bottom lip out, thinking. "Yeah, you said you grabbed it from the hardware store. You were worried about the candy cane hairdo, since you were on your way to get married—"

I stepped forward, cutting him off, "So we weren't married yet. Was I wearing a dress?"

"No." His head shifted slowly from one side to the other in a nod. "You were dressed like you are now."

"Okay." My mind raced. "So, now we know we went to the general store and got that Rudolph, then came here, got your head shaved, got a dog, and then what? Did we say where we were going?"

"You were going to get married but wanted a suit for the dog. I recommended the only clothing store that would be open that late. It's a vintage-inspired boutique called Aubergine's. I wished you congratulations, and you all three ran out together."

My eyes fled to Nick's as my heart dropped what felt like a foot. As much as I've been dying to get married since I was a little girl, *it was never supposed to happen like this!* My eyes filled with tears of dread because I didn't want confirmation that I wasted my wedding on a *Holidaze*. I managed a hard swallow as I dug for strength. "I guess we need to go to Aubergine's next, right?"

Nick's eyes stayed cemented on mine as he eased off the barber chair, heading toward the door. "I think so." A bolt of lightning zapped through me, and suddenly the only thought I had in my head was "am I looking at my husband?"

Ten

Nick

"We knocked out the whole haircut, and dog mystery in one stop," I burbled as we rushed toward the clothing store, the dog still in tow even though we never invited him. "It would be nice if I could wrap this up, solve the marriage thing, and find Santa at the next stop." I kept my gaze forward as I was now suffering from a severe case of Charlotte-centered opia. I couldn't look her in the eye anymore. My best friend for years. I felt like such a failure because I let all this get out of control.

In my dreams, I had married Charlotte a thousand times but never like this. I had hoped to give her the wedding she had always talked about, with family, friends, and a big church ceremony. Remorse was all over her face, causing shame to pour over me, as if I had somehow taken advantage of her, which was the last thing I had ever wanted to do. My heart sank. Clearly, we took a fun joke way too far, and now Charlotte was disappointed.

How was I ever going to fix this?

Deep guilt flooded my heart, and I avoided Charlotte's direct gaze like the plague. Not because I had lost any love for her, but I had lost respect for myself. Yet, I was determined to push forward and make everything better.

"Right in here." Charlotte motioned to the Victorian home branded as a vintage clothing store, and my heart sank even lower.

I maintained my queasy grin, leading the way into the house that smelled rather welcoming, like warm cinnamon. A young woman with tall hair who looked like she should be working in high-end fashion and not behind the counter of a small clothing store, stood, folding a stack of sweaters. She smiled sweetly at us, did a double-take, and her eyes flashed with recognition. She dropped the sweater mid-fold. "Good morning you two! How are you?" Her voice rang with cheer, so much that you'd think we were her beloved family members.

"Good morning," Charlotte greeted her, like we were casual shoppers bored on a Saturday. I wasn't sure where Charlotte's new composure came from, but if I had to guess I would say it was forced. "We were wondering if you remembered seeing us yesterday."

"Do I remember you?" The woman's smile stretched wide across her face, as if recalling her favorite memory. "I'll remember you two for the rest of my life. It's not every day I have to fit a dog for something."

Everything about this day had felt so emotionally heavy, but the visual of us in here trying to dress a giant dog forced me to smile back at her. "I bet that was a little crazy to see."

"I loved it." She shook her head a little wistfully. "It was so adorable seeing you both—" Her voice dropped. "Wait, you don't remember?"

Charlotte gently shook her head. "We are retracing our steps to see if people can fill us in, but yeah, we are both missing some of the memories about yesterday."

"Oh, well, let's see if I can help." Her eyes fled to the left, as if she was thinking. "You came in and said you were getting married and needed a tux for yourself and for your best man. The dog tux was an odd request, and we settled on a bowtie. You stayed about an hour, then you were off to the chapel." She lifted her shoulders and beamed a grin at us. "Other than dressing the dog, I don't recall anything out of the ordinary. It was so sweet to see you both so excited and how much in love you were."

"Love—" Charlotte choked, raising a hand to her chest, bracing herself.

Seeing Charlotte's immediate response, noticeably upset at the store clerk thinking we were in love, punched me in the gut, and I had to suck in air to keep from wincing. Obviously, I hadn't for a moment thought we'd married out of anything more than this weird Holidaze thing that came over us, but to hear Charlotte gasp for air at the thought of her loving me, burned like blue fire.

I'd said it before, and I would say it my whole life, but I honestly believed one of the most painful experiences one can go through is to fall in love with someone first . . . and then suffer through the wait, wondering when or *if* they will ever see you. Despite my internal suffering, I placed my palm on Charlotte's forearm, giving it a soft squeeze. "Are you okay?"

She nodded, but never lowered the palm still covering her chest. That small gesture did the most to tell what she was really feeling. I could see the reverberation in the cringe on her face. For the first time since I had fallen in love with her, I started to wonder if maybe I was *not* waiting for her to see me.

Maybe I was wasting my time?

If she had even a tiny seed of affection for me, she wouldn't act like she could pass out from the mere suggestion of her loving me. My hand still lingered on her arm, but she didn't look at me. "I think I'm fine." Her cadence was off, belying her statement.

Distrust flooded my heart, and I had to turn on my heel, hiding my face from both of these women, because I couldn't bear the scorn. It was one thing for Charlotte not to see me as partner material, but I had always been her friend. I didn't deserve to be lied to. I took a step away from her, letting my thoughts boil up. *Maybe this Holidaze needed to happen?* I'd been waiting for Charlotte so long I never even considered anyone else. I had put her on this pedestal, and I never allowed anyone to even come close.

Maybe this was what I needed to see for me to truly know it was never going to happen?

Some people have lightbulb moments, making everything clear. This was sort of like that, but everything instantly got dark. A true gut-punch moment, and I was done believing this waiting game would ever pay off. "It doesn't seem like we are going to learn anything else here," I called back to her as I headed toward the door, ready to get this whole thing over, and put it behind us. "Let's keep moving." I stuck my hand up in a wave and called to the lady, "Thanks for your help."

Charlotte echoed me with another thank you, and a scuffle came from behind me, and judging from the number of scattered footfalls I guessed I had both Charlotte, and the dog still in tow. After only a few short steps outside, Charlotte questioned, "Do you think we should name the dog?"

"He's not ours to name," I grumpily rebutted, because I was on a mission to get this day over. I definitely didn't want to do anything to help remember it, like naming this loyal companion. That wasn't going to help anything.

"That's the thing. *He* thinks he's ours."

I shot Charlotte an *are-you-kidding-me* look. "He can be our buddy for the weekend, but, let's get real. What are we going to do with a dog? I can't bring him back to New

York, and you said you have no idea how to care for a dog." My voice came out disgruntled, and not at all how I usually speak to Charlotte. She must have sensed my annoyance, because she dropped the conversation by looking away.

"Here's the church," I half muttered, as I took long strides. Charlotte had to do a walking-running pattern to keep up with me. Maybe that made me a jerk, but I was so disgusted with myself for wasting years of my life being naïve, that I couldn't shut down my new attitude. Who knows, maybe being a jerk would work well in my favor? You know what they say? Nice guys finish last. I wasn't trying to find out how long nice guys had to wait to get last place.

Yep, it was time to try a bolder approach with women, taking a cue from my dad. Tightening salsa jars worked for him.

We walked past the church entrance, heading toward the back to an attached residence, not slowing until we stood at the doorstep. I knocked several times before a white-haired, stout man with a swollen belly opened the door.

"Hello again," he said in a welcoming voice, his gaze wafting from Charlotte and back to me. My heart rate sped up upon seeing him recognize us.

There was no turning back.

A wave of nausea soared through my body, spiraling through my extremities, making them tremble with anxiety. Yet again, my exasperation was stoked beyond my control, and I had to grab the doorframe to stop from wobbling.

No it wasn't a new illness or even low blood sugar. It was *Zenozyne. Time was pounding away, like a drum I could hear in my ear.* It was getting faster and spinning around me until I couldn't mentally keep up with the tempo anymore. I stumbled backward, but nothing broke my fall.

Eleven

Charlotte

I blinked, and the next second Nick was laid out on the ground with the dog licking his cheek. I don't remember swooping to his side, but I was instantly squeezing his hand.

"Maybe he needs some water?" the chaplain sounded as if he was about to embark on a fun science experiment.

"It's been a stressful day." I eased into my word choices. "We weren't planning on getting married. I mean, we joked about it, but it was still a surprise for both of us."

The chaplain's brow evened out. "But you didn't get married."

I was fairly certain that gurgling came from Nick. It wasn't a choking, but not exactly living his best life sort of noise. From his position of holding the floor flat, his hand flew up like an astute student trying to get his teacher's attention. "Excuse me? Can you say that again?"

The chaplain's gaze swept to Nick. "You never got married." He gazed back to me. "You showed up, dressed in wedding apparel, and asked, but you didn't have any paperwork. I explained that this chapel doesn't operate like Vegas where you can just get hitched. There must be a license."

Nick sprang to a seated upright position, eyes glued to the chaplain, and almost sang out, "You're telling me nothing happened!"

The chaplain raised his shoulders, holding them up in pause. "I can't say what happened after, but I can say you didn't get married in my chapel. I told you to go to the courthouse on Monday for your papers."

"Wow." I stared forward, feeling foolish about everything now. *Of course, you can't just get legally married.* I had overreacted, and embarrassed heat flushed across my cheeks.

"I'm guessing you were expecting other news." The chaplain must have sensed the growing awkwardness, and tacked on a polite smile. "I'll leave you two alone to chat." He bowed his head and backed into his house, closing the door.

Nick scampered to his feet, joining me at my side. His face was paler than normal, but he looked mostly functional. Actually, he looked relieved. "That was great news," he said loudly.

"Right," I added in a soft tone as I mulled over everything. It made sense we couldn't get married. We had gotten caught in the rush of the moment, and I understood that on a logical level. The not logical thing I couldn't understand was, why, now that I learned we didn't get married, did this look of relief on Nick's face make my heart feel like it was suddenly cracked wide open? I stared back at Nick, feeling like a fool for hurting, because clearly this whole thing had been a stupid misunderstanding that should never have happened in the first place.

My heart tensed up, squeezing into a hard knot. If I had to explain what happened next, I would say it felt like the thinnest outside layer ripped wide open, and I didn't doubt I had some level of internal bleeding. I held Nick's gaze as if seeing him for the first time. A yearning sensation washed through me, and I was left feeling a pull, and complete devastation that we hadn't gotten married. I was still staring, slack jawed, fighting back budding tears when Nick interrupted my thoughts.

"I know we still have to find Santa," Nick's started in his back-to-normal tone, "but I'm suffering from thirstivation—" Cutting himself off, he held up his hand in a stop motion and rushed to add, "I do not want to go back to the Harbor Inn—that's the *last* thing we need—but would you want to grab a bite to eat at The Grove?"

The dog jumped at Nick's leg at the mere sound of food, obviously adding his yes vote. All of a sudden I understood why people like pets, despite how much work there were. It's like you could be having the worst day ever, and they still bring you a reason to smile.

Not having eaten anything all day, I should have been starving, but I had been fueled by adrenaline. Now that I learned we weren't married, the adrenaline had taken a noticeable plunge, but I wasn't hungry. Nick looked so obviously relieved; it made my disappointment spiral out of control. I didn't want him to pick up on it, so I lied, "Yeah." I forced myself to smile enough, though I had no idea why it was so hard. "I could eat," I added as I turned on my heel, and marched across the street.

What was wrong with me? I had received perfect news. I should be feeling loads of relief, but that was not the case.

I was completely devastated.

Twelve

Nick

We sat in the back of The Grove, in a booth perfect for just two. Like all the other businesses in town, this place was decked out with Christmas garland on the long counter, and Christmas music filled the air. They never said anything about not bringing the dog in, and he wasn't one to wait to be invited. He smashed in next to me, like he was a person having a regular Saturday lunch. "That dog has candy cane breath," I said, my words rolled out casually over the top of my menu as I thought about how he woke me up. You'd think it would have been disgusting to have a dog slobber all over your face, but his breath was quite pleasant.

Charlotte snickered while she set her menu face down in front of her. "He certainly has an affinity for them."

A young woman wearing a Grove T-shirt, and a cheerleader-high ponytail strolled up to our table and motioned to Charlotte's discarded menu. "Do you know what you want?"

"Yeah, I always get the same thing." Charlotte returned her menu to the waitress. "A cheeseburger, no bun, extra pickles, and BBQ sauce."

The waitress offered one of those efficient nod, and turned to me. "And you?"

I briefly glanced over the selection before I gave up. "A burger sounds good. I might just have to make that two, but I'll have the bun on mine please." A sudden wave of heavy breathing tickled the side of my face, and without having to look over, I corrected myself. "Or make it three. Our buddy wants one, too." I handed my menu back, tacking on, "And some waters please."

"You got it." She spun on her heel and left us sitting in a rare awkward silence. Usually, the time I spent with Charlotte was filled with excitement, and we never ran out of things to say. However, today was different. I supposed finding out we weren't married was the best outcome, but something inside of me felt hollow.

Maybe it was the start of me finally letting her go? Boy, I never expected that's what I'd be thinking about today. I had looked forward to this weekend all year, and now it was clouded with a heaviness in my heart. The waitress came back with our waters, and I quickly took a drink, thankful to have the refreshment. My whole body seemed parched, and I chugged almost the entire glass. Charlotte didn't seem to notice, as she was busy playing with the dog by making little finger races across the table. She was smiling again, something she hadn't done much all morning.

The dog was better at making her happy than I was.

Clearing my throat, I asked, "How's your hip? You seem to be doing better."

Her lashes fluttered before she answered. "I had forgotten, so it must not be too bad."

"I can see how you forgot," I teased sarcastically. "It's not like we haven't had anything else to think about."

"Right?" Her smile spread across her face, but it didn't reach her eyes. She couldn't fool me. Although she was acting as if she was in a better mood, something was still bothering her.

The waitress returned with our food, and we dug in but something about this morning had left me seeing more clearly than I had been. Charlotte took her first bites of food, and a pleased grin grew on her face, something about that smile infuriated me.

She has to know I love her.

Didn't she wonder why I never had a girlfriend? It's not that I was that smooth and could totally hide this from her. She looked up from her food, her eyes catching mine, and she seemed startled. "Is something wrong with your burger?"

"Nah." I had been starving ten minutes ago, but now my mind was far too focused to care about food. Before I lost my nerve, I started in a firm voice. "Question for you."

"What's that?" She took another bite of her burger patty from her fork, chewing with her eyes steady on mine.

"Did you ever think about . . . you know." I wanted to ask if she ever thought about *me*, but the word was stuck on the tip of my tongue like it was holding on for dear life, afraid to fall out of my mouth. "E-Er," I stuttered, my tongue suddenly feeling fat, like a giant puffed marshmallow I couldn't get a word over.

Charlotte set her fork down, tilting her head. "What are you thinking about?"

I opened my mouth wide, ready to spew my rant about how I had loved her for years. I'd been waiting to be seen, but now I figured out I had wasted my life, but my planet-sized tongue plug barricaded all of that in. I was left staring as if I was caught doing something wrong, but nothing was wrong with my feelings toward Charlotte.

Nothing had ever felt wrong about Charlotte.

As much as I had sworn to let her go, I felt drawn to her. I had always felt a deep connection with her, and something inside gnawed at my throat, telling me not to give up yet.

Not without a fight.

It seemed odd timing, but my mind rewound back to that note I had found in the gazebo with her writing. This weekend had not gone how I had planned, but maybe it wasn't too late?

An idea flashed through my mind, and I couldn't wait another second. "I was thinking about running an errand really quick," I said, acting indifferently. "Do you mind hanging out here until I get back?"

Her eyes dropped to my basket of uneaten food, and she pinned a perplexed expression on her face. "Um, sure."

"I'll be super quick." I scooted out of the booth, adrenaline fueling my feet again. "Stay right here." I waved toward the booth, spun on my heel, and sped out the door.

I raced down the street, hoping I wasn't too late. This could go one of two ways. It could be insanely awkward, so much so that she might not want to talk to me again or . . . it could be the start of everything.

Thirteen

Charlotte

"Where did you say you went?" I followed Nick back to the gazebo. I didn't even have to check, but I knew from the sound of loud, measured pants behind me, the dog followed us.

"I asked around to see where Santa would be." Nick's tone was a tad suspicious when he tacked on, "I knew your hip was bothering you, and I didn't want you to have to traipse all over town. I figured I could scope him out to save you the hassle."

He was mostly right about my hip. I'd been busy all day, and that kept my mind off of it, but now that I was walking again, I could tell I was brewing up a bruise. Careful to lean most of my weight on my good leg, I hobbled back through Main Street. It was December in Vermont, which meant short days, and the sun had started to tuck itself away for the night. A cloud canopy darkened the sky even more, and it did everything to make the downtown

Christmas lights pop. If I had to guess where Santa was tonight, I'd say he'd be downtown for sure. "Oh, did you find him?"

"I was told he liked to hang out by the Christmas tree for pictures."

"That makes sense," I said, matter-of-factly.

Nick was always the perfect gentleman, the guy who would walk behind me or beside me, but never a hair in front. If we walked on the sidewalk, he always took the side near the street. It was something I always loved about him, because none of the guys I ever hung around with understood old-fashioned chivalry. In a way, it reminded me of my dad. I found myself smiling as I thought about how my dad would fully approve of Nick, which would be a huge win because my dad was a hard sell when it came to the men I dated.

Wait, where'd that come from?

I startled, pinching my lips together, trying to hold back more crazy thoughts as it had been such a long day. With so much commotion, I was thinking the most random and impossible things.

As we neared the gazebo, Nick's steps slowed even more. So much so, our snail pace became a bit irritating. I stretched my neck out, scanning for a sign of Santa.

Nothing.

I glanced back at Nick, ready to shrug, but Nick didn't return my gaze. Instead, he remained focused on the Gazebo, specifically the ceiling where Christmas lights glittered. Wait, no, not Christmas lights— I took the last steps up to the gazebo steps, and stood in awe at what was before me.

Stars, like the kind you buy in bags at the store and stick to your bedroom ceiling, had been plastered all over the top of the gazebo. They spelled out Carpe Diem.

My confusion lifted when I noticed the smile Nick had for me. It clearly said he was the one responsible for the stars. This wasn't the first time he'd done something just to make me smile, but this was *different*. I didn't recognize it but I felt a tingling deep in my gut.

I turned in a circle, admiring the stars from different angles. "What's this all about?" Even the dog seemed in awe as he walked to the center and laid down, staring up.

He stuffed his hands in his jean's pocket, and looked at me with a bit of a sideways glance. "I'm taking a cue from your dad."

"Seize the day?" I hiked a brow, feeling lost, maybe a little angst.

He took a small step toward me, and motioned to the pocket in his coat, which I was still wearing. "I found something earlier and I stuffed it in there."

"Huh?" I was put off by the sudden change of conversation, because I still didn't quite understand the sticky stars, but I stuffed my hand into his pocket and dug around until I found a small piece of paper and pulled it out.

All I want for Christmas is to find my husband. And if you can't do that this year, can you at least send a sign that I shouldn't give up. A shooting star or

"That's my handwriting," I thought out loud, but I didn't remember writing it. At this point I wasn't surprised. It wasn't the dumbest thing I had done in the last twenty-four hours. Nick reached out, touched the note, letting his finger linger under the words shooting star. With his free hand, he motioned to the sticky stars above us. "I was trying to think of a way to tell you something, but . . . yeah. I guess, I don't want to wait to make the memories."

He took another step forward, now only an arm's reach in front of me. "I was thinking about how a lot of times we think our best day is going to be the day we get married or the day we get a huge raise. After spending a good part of our day thinking I'd never remember our wedding, I thought the best day of my life will probably be some random Saturday, where you and I walk around town, doing the most basic things, like we do every year when we meet here in Mapleton. Once I thought that, I wasn't sad about not having my wedding memories." He paused, and stared at his feet, a slight tint in his cheek showed he was nervous.

My mouth dropped open, as I realized he was trying to do something really sweet. I still wasn't *exactly* sure where he was going with this whole thing, but it had a swoony

Christmas movie feel going on, and my heart was swelling bigger with each word he said.

"I don't know if that means I'm ready to skip the big moments," he finally continued, "and just be basic all day, but I'm happiest when I am hanging out with you. All day I had this feeling, like I had failed you, and all these terrible thoughts ran through my head. Once I realized we never got married, I thought about how spending today retracing our steps made the best memories ever, even if we didn't feel that happy while it was happening. I know I'll always remember this day as Kairosclerosis."

I hiked both brows, hoping he'd give me the definition of this word.

His eyes swept to the stars on the roof, and then back to my face, joining with mine. "It means the moment when you realize you are happy, and for me, I realized I was happy when I was being basic with you." Wagging his head to the side, he tacked on, "Sure, I had a few random waves of nausea, and a panic attack that caused me to faint but, in the end, I think that only added to the memory."

He was giving me a look, I'd never seen from him, but I didn't have to think twice what it meant. He bit one side of his lip and met my eyes directly with a penetrating stare. A shiver ran down my spine. This look only ever meant one thing. It's the look that happens on the cusp of a moment that's about to turn romantic. We were at a crossroads where everything could change, and a flame ignited inside me. It kindled into a fire that roared through me and didn't stop until it engulfed my heart.

I can't believe I had missed who was right in front of me all these years. I had been thinking out of tune, and now I was finally on the same wavelength as Nick. I was about to reply when I was interrupted by a hearty, "Ho, ho, ho."

"Santa!" Nick and I exclaimed, more excited than kids on Christmas morning. Santa was driving past us in a horse-drawn sleigh, and each horse had antlers tied to their heads and whinnied quietly. Nick and I scampered down the steps of the gazebo out to the street, arms flailing like we were trying to win a foot race, screaming, "We have to talk to you!"

Nick ran until he caught up to the sleigh. Santa pulled back on the reins, halting his reindeer. "Santa!" Nick repeated, his breath now coming out in huffs. "There's been a mistake."

Santa peered down his wire-rimmed glasses, a smile gracing his lips. "Don't tell me you want your letters back."

My bum hip finally allowed me to catch up, and I joined Nick. Before I could ask what Santa meant about the letters, Nick continued, "I'm afraid we made a large donation last night to Toys for Tots, and as much as we think it's a great cause, I was hoping we had a chance to return some of that donation. We got a little carried away."

The smile that had budded on Santa's lips grew into one filled with so much joy as he reached into his pocket and pulled out a few slips of paper. "Let's see my list here," he said to himself as he appeared to read from the sheets. I know the toys you are referring to, but I don't recall them being your donation. I distinctly remember I took care of that."

I started to argue, wanting to explain what the lady at the hardware store had said, but Santa gave us a wink. This wasn't just any wink. It appeared to have a twinkle spark at the corner of his eye, making his whole face light up like a glistening magical mirage. Before we could speak, he reached down and handed Nick the papers.

"These are your letters to me. Normally, I keep them for insurance purpose, so people can't complain when I bring them exactly what they asked for, but in this case, I think these will help you get what you need better than I can." His gaze acknowledged us one more time, before he pulled back on his reins, chuckled, and called out, "Merry Christmas, Nick and Charlotte!" and he drove off.

"That was . . . strange." I eyed Santa as his sleigh moved away so fast it appeared to be floating, and disappeared down the street. I hadn't the faintest clue why he thought this letter had belonged to me. I hadn't written a letter to Santa since I was nine years old. I started to turn on my heel to head back to the lodge, ready to call the credit card companies to see what I was on the hook for, when Nick looked up from the letter, his eyes wide. "You need to read this."

An immediate sense of dread filled my chest. "What's going on now?"

"Get your note out again." He flashed the paper at me, and I could see the bottom was torn off.

I dug back into his pocket, grabbed the sheet and held the two together. *It was a perfect match.* "Oh, wow, what did I write this time?" My voice barely squeaked out.

He pushed both papers toward me. "Read it."

Inhaling, I took a long breath, drinking in courage as I snatched it from his hand and read in a monotone voice.

"Or maybe if this is too hard for you to find me a husband on your own, I'll give you some hints: He's tall, with perfect manners just like my dad, that way my dad would approve. He makes me laugh even when we do the most random day things. He's smart and always knows how to make me smile. He uses rare words that only he would know—" My voice dropped off.

My heart constricted.

I did not just read that . . .

As if to confirm what was right in front of me, one tiny snowflake glittered down onto my letter, landing perfectly on the word "rare." Holding my breath, I waited for the snowflake to melt, but it stayed frozen, glistening back at me.

There's clearly only one person who had the weird ob-session with rare words.

He was standing right in front of me.

"This is weird," I squawked out, feeling confused, but not-like-it-was-written-at-the-Geneva-Convention confused. More like why-am-I-the-last-to-know confused?

Nick pushed the other paper forward. "Now read this one."

I tried to take it without looking at him, but his eyes had this crazy magnetic pull. Like an impenetrable force, and my gaze glued to his. It was near-impossible to tear my eyes away to read the paper, but my burning curiosity made me do it.

"I don't need a soulmate, just someone who fits perfectly under my chin."

My eyes instantly stung with tears begging me not to hold back anymore. There couldn't be a clearer sign pointing me to Nick. A spiral of warm wind snuck behind me and pushed me forward. I struggled not to stumble, but I had gotten the hint. With the letter still in hand, I stepped forward, closing the gap between us until I was right under his chin. "You know," I started slowly, not feeling scared at all. "I refuse to believe in soulmates, but the way my forehead butts up neatly into the nook below your chin is . . . perfect."

Somewhere in the distance, we heard a jolly voice ring out, "Merry Christmas Nick and Charlotte. Ho, ho, ho."

Goosebumps dotted my spine. "You don't think that was a *real* Santa?"

"Nah." Nick brushed my comment away, while stealing another look at the night sky. "He was clearly pretending."

"Totally pretending," I rushed to add because I didn't want Nick to think I was weird, and actually believed in things like Santa.

"Charlotte," Nick's voice was soft, beckoning me to look up at him. I arched my chin. My eyes found his, but immediately they dropped to his lips. I parted my lips and met his in our first kiss. His lips were soft, his breath—candy cane peppermint, but his arms that wrapped me into his Nick nook, were *everything*. I pulled back from our kiss, we joined hands and sauntered back toward the lodge, laughing about the day.

The dog perfectly in tow.

Soft Christmas music pipped out over the main square and as we passed the general store, the lady who had helped us stood near the window, pulling the curtains shut. She noticed us walk past. Her lips turned up slightly at the corners and she winked like she was holding a secret only she was privy to.

Epilogue
The next fall . . .

"Matching turtlenecks," Nick's inventory voice rolled out, like he was taking command of an important mission.

I grinned at how adorable he looked in the mustard-colored sweater under his coat. It wasn't my color, but I'd been waiting so long to make these memories, I'd wear a gorilla suit at this point if it made for a cute Christmas card. I giggled, and called back, "Check."

"Pumpkin spice lattes with a skosh of whipped cream," he continued in his roll call voice. He had warned me this morning that he had a big date planned for us, but never in my wildest dreams did I think he'd combine every perfect date I had ever hinted I wanted and throw them into one. Well, to be fair, not all of them, because that would be impossible but enough to make it memorable. We were all about making the most memories.

"Check." I called back to him as I held up my cup, lightly tapping it with his in a toast. He held out his other arm, hooking my arm into his as we headed out of the Coffee Loft.

"Adorable dog," he added to his list.

Neither of us had to check behind as we knew he'd be in tow. After having spent the weekend with us over Christmas break, we didn't have the heart to turn him out into the streets. Since neither of us were equipped to house a dog in our regular lives, we left him with Nick's parents, but we couldn't be happier to be reunited this weekend. He seemed to respond like he did the first time we met, never leaving our sides.

"Buddy is here. Check," I called back.

"Pumpkin patch," he called out again. This time, a chuckle slipped through his lips.

"On our way." I smirked at him, my heart swelling with all the perfect picture moments we would create today. I wanted to fulfill my promise to my dad not to wait for the perfect day, but to take the memories as they came, and accept the imperfections.

Nick and I had spent the last eight months doing the long-distance relationship thing, with him commuting from New York, and me from Texas. Nothing about it was perfect, but I accepted that because it was still amazing. We were both sick of the distance, though. I had visited him a few times in New York, and it didn't feel right to me. He came to see me in Texas, and that didn't feel right either. As far as jobs for us, the doors weren't opening as we needed them to.

This weekend we decided to come back to Mapleton, hoping to gain some clarity. We strolled, with arms linked, down Main Street until we arrived at the enormous colonial house on the corner that said Mapleton B&B. It had a For Sale sign in front of it, and I couldn't help but take in a whimsical sigh. "I didn't even know Mapleton had a Bed and Breakfast. How cute is that? We should totally buy this B&B and move back to Mapleton to run it," I half-joked.

I glanced at Nick, and he had a super serious expression I'd never seen before. I halted, and an immediate rush fled through my veins. Tilting my head slowly toward him, feeling like I was about to traipse all over something sacred, I whispered, "What's wrong?"

"I was going to wait until the perfect time to give you this." He slipped off his jacket and offered it to me. The look on his face remained stoic.

I quirked a brow, not demeaning his kind gesture, but it wasn't cold enough that I needed a jacket on top of my wool sweater. "Thanks for the offer but I'm not cold."

"It's not about the jacket." Nick continued to hold out his coat. "But it's more about living in the moment."

"What?" I quipped, while wondering if me wearing his jacket had a sentimental thing he was holding onto? As I eyed it, a little suspiciously now, I recognized it as the jacket

I had worn last year when I had gotten mine wet. "Is . . . there a reason I need to wear that jacket if I'm *not* cold?"

"Maybe I have a confession." His lips pursed out thoughtfully before he added, "And I think it's easier to show it to you."

"Okay . . ." I took the jacket, resisting the urge to sling it over my shoulder just to tease him. Instead, I dutifully put it on, and peered back at him. "Now what?"

Chuckling, his gaze shifted above my head while he tugged at the collar of his turtleneck, but he didn't tell me what was up with the jacket, so I repeated, "What do I do now that I'm wearing it? Do you want to take a ridiculous selfie with me? Or is this when I finally bust out my duck lips?" I smashed my lips together and pretended to pose by hoisting my hands on my hips. Then in a second pose, just to be sassy, I pushed my hip out and brought my hands higher. When I did, my hand brushed against a lump in the pocket. I barely noticed it and would have shrugged it off, but Nick sucked in such an explosive breath I thought he was about to sneeze. "What was that?" I asked, my gaze cementing on him.

Sometimes in life you have a rare moment where it feels like you can speak an entire conversation by studying the nuances in someone's eyes. This was one of those moments. Each tiny flicker of Nick's iris was so slow and deliberate, like the rhythm of a song I memorized. As I stared deeper into his gaze, I felt a slow ripple of emotion gather in my gut, and then gently flow up, building strength in a wave that made its way to my heart.

"So, my confession is . . ." Nick's words were measured, soft, and filled with flirtation. "I wore that jacket last time we were here."

"I remember that," I stated flatly.

"And," he tipped his head toward me, pausing briefly before saying, "we both remember what happened last year, but I had planned this huge weekend . . ." He dug into his bottom lip with his teeth and slowly let his lip roll back out. "I was pretty lame, but I had planned to profess my feelings to you, and I was serious about wanting to show you *exactly* how I felt about you."

"Okay . . ." I whispered. I didn't want to break the seriousness of Nick's tone. His piercing gaze sent a cold sweat to dot my lower back. I wouldn't say he hadn't said nice things to me before, because he was always a sweetheart, but the intensity of his gaze had me curling my toes.

"For once in my life, I don't have the perfect word," he blurted out and jerked his hand toward his coat. His volume leveled up to a frustrated notch. "Can you just check that pocket!"

Springing my head back from the sudden change of subject, I was startled. "Ah, sure." I fumbled for his pocket, reaching my hand in slowly at first but then when I didn't find anything, I dug deeper into the large pocket until my fingers grazed something velvety . . . a tiny box.

Tears welled in my eyes before I even got the box out. I couldn't look at it, though, and whisked it forward, handing it quickly over to Nick with my eyes pinned shut. "Are you serious?" I squealed, while wiping the corner of my eye.

Nick set our latte cups on the curb, stood up straight, and rotated the box in his hand, positioning it perfectly, like he was both teasing and torturing me. "I spent the last decade waiting for the perfect moments to tell you how I felt and to do all the things. Last year, I learned I wasted a whole lot of time worrying instead of making memories." He opened the box, flashing a solitaire diamond ring at me.

I honestly only got a glimpse of it before tears clouded my vision. My heart motored up to unnatural speed, and I barely heard what he said next.

"I was worried that I wouldn't get the perfect ring or say the perfect thing, but something I learned this year is that the perfect moment with you is *always now.*"

Pinching the ring between his index finger and thumb, he removed the ring from the box, and held it out, while taking a knee. "Charlotte." He paused, locking his eyes with mine. He didn't have to say the words because I read everything in the inflections in his eyes, but I stayed quiet as he went on, "I cannot waste another moment *waiting* for perfection because together *is* perfection."

Time seemed to slow, so much so that I could feel the rhythmic beating of my heart reminding me that I was living through this moment, making a memory. Nick took my hand in his and slipped the ring on my finger. As he smiled at me, with that brilliant smile that told me I was everything to him, I held my breath and waited for the last part.

"Charlotte Bradbury, will you marry me?"

I was about to flutter my lashes at him and swoon when a scuffle from behind us broke out, and frantic barking sounded off. Buddy took off after an alley cat, spilling Nick's coffee all over the sidewalk, *ruining our perfect moment*. I bit back a giggle, and I caught Nick's exasperated expression.

I knew in my heart the catfight didn't actually ruin the moment. It was the very thing that perfected our imperfect proposal.

Nick chuckled, haphazardly motioned to my hand again. "About what I was saying?"

"Yes," I simpered back, never happier. "I can't think of anyone else I'd rather live a more perfect, imperfect life with. Of course, I will marry you."

Nick slid the ring on my finger and as I gazed lovingly down at it, he tilted his head toward the B&B. "We're buying that, aren't we?"

I nodded, but I couldn't say anything because the moment felt so surreal. My lips spread into a huge grin, and I tilted my head the opposite way where Buddy had run, "And totally adopting that dog."

"Oh shoot!" Nick startled, his eyes searching the street. "We can't let him run away. He might get into something."

"Like what?" I chuckled, feeling the sarcasm burn in my throat. "A Holidaze."

Nick's eyes opened even wider, and he took my hand in his, and together we took off running down the street, yelling, "Buddy, come back!"

Thank you for reading 'Tis the Season to Get Married!

For sneak peek at another book in my Christmas Shenanigan's series, **Mingle all the Way,** flip to the page after the series page.

Also, did you know Charlotte makes her debut in another book? It's called Upcycling My Rig-Pig Boss and available now: https://www.amazon.com/dp/B0BWFR4X98

Upcycling my Rig-Pig Boss is an Opposites Attract, HEA Sweet Romance with a cinnamon roll hero, and a big-hearted hippie.

About J.P. Sterling

I write wholesome stories and love all things slapstick humor and heart strings.

Aside from writing, I'm also a wife and homeschooling mom, a holistic nutritionist, a jewelry designer, a professional archivist, former college instructor and lover of all things dark chocolate.

Author Clean Code: I like to make my stories about the story and not about a bunch of profanity, mature content, or graphic violence that are only there to shock you. I write my stories to be family friendly.

Guess what amazing thing just happened?

I just launched my own private reading group on Facebook. Want to be part of my inner circle of readers? Hop in the group here: https://www.facebook.com/groups/1500850764081965

For free audio books please visit:

https://www.youtube.com/c/JpSterling

Find me on Instagram:

https://www.instagram.com/authorjpsterling/

Sign up to my free monthly newsletter to get the first look at my new books, free book offers and random updates:

https://landing.mailerlite.com/webforms/landing/q9c0v

3

Also By J.P. Sterling

Bosses and Billionaires Series (All Standalones)

Maid for my Billionaire Boss

Upcycling My Rig-Pig Boss

Marooned with My Celebrity Boss (Only Available in my private Facebook group)

Kissed by My Billionaire Boss (Coming 2024)

A Heart that Dances Series

Dancing on Broken Ankles

The Stars We See

A Heart that Dances

A Heart that Loves

Water and Stone Duet

Ruby in the Water

Lily in the Stone

Christmas Shenanigans (All Standalones)

Mingle All the Way

'Tis the Season to get Married.

The Coffee Loft Series (All Standalones)

Pardon My French Press (Coming Jan. 2024) https://www.amazon.com/dp/B0CG2NRLJ7